He winked at her. "I'm beginning to think I let the only one for me get away a long time ago."

The warmth that gushed through her was at once exhilarating and terrifying. "I'll see you tomorrow." Sasha dropped behind the wheel and closed the door before Branch could say anything else.

He watched as she backed from the drive and drove away.

Branch Holloway had always been incredibly charming. He hadn't meant what he said the way it sounded—the way her mind and body took it. Sasha was certain on that one. Being kind was one of his most well-known traits. It was as natural as breathing.

He hadn't actually meant that she had stolen his heart and ruined him for anyone else. They'd had a one-night stand after years of her pining after him.

End of story.

At least, for Branch, it had ended there.

For Sasha, that night had only been the beginning.

THE DARK WOODS

USA TODAY Bestselling Author
DEBRA WEBB

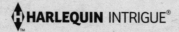

This book is dedicated to the outstanding police officers and
deputies in Winchester and Franklin County, Tennessee.
Thank you for all you do.

ISBN-13: 978-1-335-60422-4

The Dark Woods

Copyright © 2019 by Debra Webb

Recycling programs
for this product may
not exist in your area.

Printed in U.S.A.

www.Harlequin.com

Debra Webb is the award-winning *USA TODAY* bestselling author of more than one hundred novels, including those in reader-favorite series Faces of Evil, the Colby Agency and the Shades of Death. With more than four million books sold in numerous languages and countries, Debra's love of storytelling goes back to childhood on a farm in Alabama. Visit Debra at www.debrawebb.com.

Books by Debra Webb

Harlequin Intrigue

A Winchester, Tennessee Thriller

In Self Defense
The Dark Woods

Colby Agency: Sexi-ER

Finding the Edge
Sin and Bone
Body of Evidence

Faces of Evil

Dark Whispers
Still Waters

Colby Agency: The Specialists

Bridal Armor
Ready, Aim...I Do!

Colby, TX

Colby Law
High Noon
Colby Roundup

Debra Webb writing with Regan Black

Harlequin Intrigue

Colby Agency: Family Secrets

Gunning for the Groom

The Specialists: Heroes Next Door

The Hunk Next Door
Heart of a Hero
To Honor and To Protect
Her Undercover Defender

Visit the Author Profile page at Harlequin.com.

CAST OF CHARACTERS

Sasha Lenoir—The one thing she wants more than anything else is to prove her father did not murder her mother and then take his own life.

US Marshal Branch Holloway—Has a few secrets of his own but the one thing he wants right now is to help Sasha find the truth.

Leandra Brennan—Has something to hide...maybe a secret as dark as the woods surrounding Sasha's childhood home.

Jarvis Packard—No one has more to lose than the richest developer in the state.

Alfred Nelson—Was he obsessed with Sasha's mother? What secret is he keeping?

Chapter One

Sasha Lenoir struggled to keep her smile in place as her lifelong friend Audrey Anderson showed the last of the guests to the door. The gathering after her grandmother's funeral was a tradition as old as time, and Sasha had managed to muddle through the event without embarrassing herself by bursting into tears. As the social requirements of the day drew to an end, however, her nerves had grown ragged and her wherewithal dwindled.

She needed to close herself away in a quiet room for a few hours to recharge, to collect her emotions and tuck them neatly away once more. She had spent many years sharpening her skills at controlling her reactions and feelings. Despite the pressure or the insurmountable odds, any crisis manager worth her salt would never allow the slightest crack in her carefully constructed veneer for the rest of the world to see.

But today had been different. Today was personal. The only remaining family member, besides her daughter, she had left in this world was now gone. Dead and buried. There was no one left to ask about her history. No one to remind her of all she had overcome, become and could do in the future despite that history.

Life would never be the same.

Viola Simmons had been more than a mere grandmother. She had been mother, father, sibling, best friend, confidante, cheerleader and, most important, the keeper of the faith. Not once had she ever lost faith in Sasha or let her down in any way. The sweet, brave lady had believed in Sasha when she barely believed in herself. She had picked up the shattered pieces of their lives and soldiered on when she had every right to want to give up.

There was a gaping hole in Sasha's life and in her heart now.

"I should stay tonight," Audrey offered as she entered the drawing room once more. "You shouldn't be alone."

Sasha dredged up a weary smile for her old friend. "I appreciate everything you've done, Rey. I'm not sure I would have been able to pull this off to my grandmother's standards without you, but right now alone is exactly what I need to be."

Everyone close to Audrey had always called her Rey. Nicknames were a mainstay of Southern culture. When Sasha was a small child, her parents—even her grandmother—had called her Sassy. By age twelve, no one dared to do so—not without the fear of a black eye or a bloody nose. Only once in her career as a top crisis manager in New York City had Sasha's childhood nickname surfaced. She had quashed that errant leak in a heartbeat.

"Are you sure?" Rey's face lined with worry. "I really hate to go and leave you in this big old house all by yourself."

Sasha hugged her arm around her old friend's and guided her to the door. "You've done more than enough." They faced each other in the entry hall. "You handled the outreach to her friends. You went over my grandmother's wishes and arranged the entire service at DuPont's with hardly a nod from me. You organized the lovely gathering here afterward. You've gone above and beyond already. Go home, kick your shoes off and have a glass of wine—or two…or three. Snuggle with Colt."

They laughed together. But instead of sounding happy, it seemed sad. It was the end of an era and Sasha suspected Rey was thinking of her own mother, who wasn't getting any younger and whose health had been plagued by dementia. Time stopped for no one and it felt as if it was slipping away far too fast.

Rey sighed. "The service was beautiful. I know your g'ma would have been proud." Rey shook her head. "It's such a shame about Mr. DuPont. I can't believe a close colleague of his daughter's murdered him. I'm certain she must be completely devastated."

The news of the DuPont murder had rocked the small town of Winchester, Tennessee. DuPont Funeral Home had served the community for more than a hundred and fifty years. Edward had been the fourth generation DuPont undertaker. His daughter Dr. Rowan DuPont was now the fifth. Strange, Sasha realized, the DuPont family's history was littered with as much tragedy as her own. Rowan's identical twin sister drowned when she was twelve and a few months later their mother committed suicide. Worse, her mother hanged herself in the funeral home and Rowan was the one to find her.

"I was surprised to hear she'd decided to return to Winchester and take over the funeral home." Like Sasha, Rowan DuPont had carved out a good life and a successful career elsewhere. With her father's murder she had apparently made the decision to give up everything to come home and take over the family business. There was likely more to Rowan's decision than what the media had covered. Whatever her reasons, Sasha applauded her courage. It took guts to come home after a tragedy and to start over.

Particularly with the guilt of her father's murder hanging over her like a dark cloud.

"Life has a way of sending us down a different path sometimes," Rey said almost to herself.

Sasha inwardly cringed. Her friend was right; no one understood that stark fact better than Rey. A hitch in her career had brought her home to some immensely dark history of her own that just last month had surfaced for the whole world to see.

"I guess we never know what the future holds." Sasha chafed her bare arms with her hands, chasing away the sudden chill that came from deep within her bones. "Don't you find it odd that the three of us have suffered such similar tragic pasts?" Sasha shook her head. "Winchester is a small town and that's a lot of skeletons rattling around."

Rey made an agreeable sound. "I suppose every small town has its secrets."

"My grandmother probably knew them all." Sasha laughed, the sound strained despite her effort to lighten the moment. "No one was privy to more rumors and gossip than Viola Simmons."

Rey smiled. "There was something about her—an aura maybe—that made you want to spill your guts." Rey grabbed her handbag from beneath the table next to the door. "Don't forget I want to do a reflection piece on her. Everyone loved Vi. It'll be a great way to pay tribute to such an admired lady."

"She would be so honored, Rey." Sasha's grandmother would love the notoriety. "We'll get together next week and talk."

Rey paused, her hand on the door. "Does that mean you're hanging around for a few days longer than you first anticipated?"

Sasha didn't hesitate. She took the plunge. "I told my partners I would be gone for at least two weeks. If there's an emergency they know how to reach me."

"I am so glad to hear that." Rey nodded. "You should take your time and do what you need to do before you jump back into work." A frown tugged at her lips. "Will Brianne be okay with you staying so long?"

"She's having a blast with her nanny. The woman spoils her rotten."

"And," Rey pointed out, "you get some *me* time. I have a feeling that doesn't happen often."

"No kidding. I can definitely use it." Though, in truth, it was work that stole most of Sasha's time, not her precious daughter.

The two hugged for a moment and then Rey hurried to the street and the car she'd left there that morning. She'd arrived early to help Sasha get ready for the funeral. She was a good friend and Sasha genuinely appreciated her help. Three times each year Sasha had visited her grandmother—on her birthday in September, Mother's Day and at Christmas. She and Rey, on the other hand, had lunch at least every other month since Rey lived in DC—or at least she had until she suddenly rushed back to Winchester to take over the family newspaper late last year. Sasha would never in a million years have considered that Rey would move back to Winchester. Not after the way Sheriff Colt Tanner, her first love, had broken her heart when they were in high school. Not only was Rey back in her hometown, she and Colt were giving their relationship a second go. Sasha definitely had not seen that one coming, though she was immensely happy for her dear friend.

Maybe happy endings weren't a total myth after all. Certainly there was a theme going on with the whole homecoming thing.

Sasha had made her own happy ending far away from Winchester and without any help from the man she had fallen head over heels for when she was too young to understand what heartbreak was. She and Brianne were a strong, complete family. They would both miss G'ma but they still had each other.

Sasha closed the door and, out of habit, locked it. She'd lived in Manhattan for the past thirteen years. One didn't leave the door unlocked in the city. No matter that almost two decades had passed since she'd lived in Winchester, folks in her small hometown hadn't changed very much. Doors were still left unlocked more often than not and neighbors still checked on each other on a regular basis, which was the reason her grandmother had been found so quickly after her unexpected death. She hadn't come out for her newspaper. Viola Louise Simmons would never have left her newspaper lying on the porch until noon. A neighbor had noticed and knocked on the door to check on Vi, as her friends had called her.

A heart attack had taken her as she sat down for her morning tea. At eighty-three, no one could complain that Viola hadn't lived a long and productive life. Yet Sasha still grieved the loss, felt shocked at the idea that her grandmother was no longer here. She leaned against the closed door and surveyed the familiar surroundings. She had lived in this big old house from age nine until she went off to college and after that she'd spent holidays and summers here.

Growing up, this house had been more her home than any other place. Even when her parents were still alive, she was with her grandmother far more often than with them. Sasha pushed away from the door and moved along the hall, studying the family portraits and photos that had captured a place in time, curating the moment for all eternity. She stopped and stared at one portrait in particular, the last one of her with her parents before they died. Memories of the photographer urging Sasha's mother, Alexandra, to smile whispered through her mind. Her parents had both looked uncomfortable that day. But Sasha had been a kid, so she hadn't really noticed at the time. Two weeks later they were dead.

The remembered sound of gunshots blasted in her brain, making her jerk.

Sasha banished the haunting memories and walked to the kitchen. Maybe a cup of tea would settle her nerves.

She put the kettle on, lit the flame beneath it then reached instinctively to the pocket of her suit jacket and found nothing. She sighed. *Upstairs.* Her cell phone was upstairs. The device was as much a part of her as her two hands. It was never beyond reach… except for today. Out of respect for her grandmother she had left it in her room. Viola had hated cell phones. Rather than money, she had been convinced the invention of the cell phone was the root of all evil.

Sasha smiled as she took the rear staircase up to the second floor. The house was an early nineteenth-century American Foursquare. Sasha loved this place, but she wasn't sure what she would do with it. Her life was in New York and she couldn't possibly move back here. Never in a million years.

She found her cell on the bedside table in her old room. A text flashed on the screen. Sasha smiled as she responded, typing the words I miss you, too, followed by three kiss emoji. Her heart swelled. She was really glad Brianne wasn't angry with her anymore. Her daughter had been furious when Sasha told her she couldn't come to G'ma's funeral. She had school and Sasha wasn't sure how long she would need to remain in order to settle her grandmother's affairs. At least Brianne was speaking to her now. Five minutes after Sasha was out the door, her daughter was planning all the things she and her beloved nanny could do together. Twelve was a tough age. Sasha remembered it well.

Love you.

Sasha sent the text and tucked the phone into her pocket. Downstairs the kettle screamed for her attention. She could taste the bitter tang of the tea already. Her grandmother was a die-hard Earl Grey fan. Sasha compensated with an abundance of sugar and milk.

With a quick twist of the knob she doused the fluttering flame under the kettle. She grabbed a cup and the ceramic box where her grandmother stored her tea. She dropped a bag into the cup and grabbed a mitt to pour the hot water. While the tea steeped she went to the refrigerator for the milk and rounded up the sugar.

The doorbell rang, echoing its Westminster chime through the house. Hoping it wasn't another plant since the front parlor was full already, Sasha made her way to the entry hall. Rey had suggested the plants be donated to one or more of the nursing or assisted living homes in the area. First thing tomorrow a local floral shop was sending a van to collect the plants and divide them up among the three homes in the Winchester area. It was a good solution, one her g'ma would approve of. Sasha peeked beyond the drapes, didn't see anyone on the porch or in the drive. Frowning, she unlocked the door and opened it. Definitely no one on the porch or in the driveway.

When she would have turned away, she spotted the corner of a pink envelope sticking up from the mailbox hanging on the wall next to the door. Had someone dropped off a sympathy card? Maybe a neighbor who hadn't been able to make it to the service or to the gathering.

Sasha tugged the envelope from the mailbox, then went back inside and closed the door. Her name was scrawled across the front. She turned the envelope over, noted the bold *H* stamped on the flap. Her heart stumbled as she opened it. The single page inside was folded twice. Frowning, Sasha unfurled the page and read the brief note that went straight to the point and then the name signed across the bottom of the page.

There are things your grandmother should have told you...about your parents. We should talk. Arlene Holloway.

For twenty-seven years the world had believed Sasha's father had killed her mother and then himself.

Deep down she'd had questions, had doubts. But each time Sasha had broached the subject, her grandmother hugged her and said that sometimes bad things happened to good people. Her grandmother was like the policemen who came to her parents' house that night. They didn't want to listen to what a traumatized nine-year-old had to say. Two people were dead and nothing on earth was going to bring them back.

But Sasha remembered vividly what no one had wanted to believe.

She had heard at least one stranger's voice that night…maybe two. Voices that didn't belong to her mother or to her father or to anyone else she recognized.

Someone else had been in the house the night her parents died.

Chapter Two

Arlene Holloway was born and raised in Winchester. Sasha stood at the woman's front door as the sun dipped behind the trees and mountains that surrounded her hometown. Mrs. Holloway was—had been—Vi's best friend. Didn't matter that Vi was black and Arlene was white and that their childhood era had not been amenable to multicultural relationships of any sort. The two had weathered that storm and become stronger because of it. Through marriage and childbearing and widowhood Vi and Arlene had grown even closer over the years. Both had warned Sasha's mother nearly forty years ago how difficult life could potentially be if she chose to marry a white man. Alexandra had ignored the warning and married Sasha's father. Sasha had the dark curly hair of her mother and the pale skin and green eyes of her father.

More important, she had the determination and relentlessness of her grandmother. Both had served her well in the high-stakes world of celebrities and politicians where ruthless tactics and colliding egos were par for the course. Handling the high-profile issues of the rich and famous as well as the influential and powerful required a certain skill set, including fearlessness. The fearlessness as well she had inherited from her grandmother.

But for her parents, as predicted, life had been difficult and far too short.

Sasha knocked on the door a second time, and when the knob turned, her heart took another of those troubling tumbles. Was it possible that after all these years she might be on the verge of learning something new about what happened that night? If her grandmother had possessed some knowledge as to the events that unfolded that fateful night, why would she not have told Sasha years ago? The answer was easy—Viola Simmons would have done anything, gone to any lengths to protect her only grandchild. She firmly believed the past should stay in the past. Viola had wanted desperately for Sasha to move forward with no dwelling in a history that could not be changed.

But what if some aspects of it could change?

Why would Vi ignore that possibility?

The door swung inward and Sasha prepared to launch into her planned spiel about how she and Mrs. Holloway hadn't had the opportunity to properly catch up during the funeral or later at the graveside service or even at the gathering. She decided she wouldn't bring up the mysterious letter until the older woman did.

Except it wasn't eighty-five-year-old Arlene Holloway staring at Sasha when the door opened fully. It was Branch... Mrs. Holloway's grandson.

US Marshal Branch Holloway.

The boy Sasha had loved from afar since she was thirteen years old. The man she'd finally—after a decade of fostering a secret crush—made love with in his truck on the heels of having had far too much champagne at her five-year high school reunion.

The *man* who was the father of her twelve-year-old blond-haired, blue-eyed daughter.

A fact the man in question did not know.

That trademark grin spread across his handsome face—the same face she saw in her daughter every day. "Sasha Lenoir...aren't you a sight for sore eyes."

And just like that her heart melted and she wanted to lean into him the way she had that one night almost thirteen years ago. It would be so easy to cry on his wide shoulders after losing the only real parent she'd had. To lose herself in the warmth and promise of his arms and forget that she, like her grandmother had been, was on her own now, raising a child.

Except Sasha had far too much to lose to even think of going down that path. Her decision not to tell Branch about her pregnancy and the daughter she'd had nine months later had been based on fear and self-doubt during an intensely stressful time. She'd just graduated with her master's and had dozens of job interviews in front of her. Two months later she'd barely settled into her new career when she realized she was pregnant. Her life had already been far too complicated; she couldn't drag Branch into it. He was kicking butt and taking names in Chicago. There simply was no common ground for them to find for raising a child together. She'd made the decision not to tell him and her grandmother and Rey had kept her secret.

Now the decision seemed like the mistake it no doubt was. Brianne was missing out on the wonderful man who was her father and the still unmarried Branch had no idea what an amazing daughter he had helped create.

Remorse heaped onto Sasha's shoulders. What had she done?

She'd also caused her grandmother to keep that secret from her lifelong best friend. Her poor grandmother had taken that weight with her to her grave.

More guilt accumulated to the point Sasha almost sagged. But didn't.

All at once regret claimed Branch's expression. "I'm as sorry as I can be about your grandmother. I would have been at the funeral today but there was an emergency with a prisoner transfer."

Arlene had explained Branch's absence. Not that Sasha had really expected him to come to the funeral. They hadn't exactly been close friends back in school. He was two years older and had been too popular to have time for a mere human like Sasha and her friends. But he'd always been kind. Besides being incredibly handsome and spectacularly charming, one thing Branch Holloway had always been was kind. Fear abruptly clutched Sasha's heart. How kind would he be if he ever learned her secret? She had stolen a dozen years of his daughter's life from him.

She pushed the negative thoughts away. No one was better at keeping shocking secrets or neutralizing the rumors around those secrets than Sasha. They didn't call her the queen of spin doctors for nothing. As for her personal dilemma, she had made her bed; she would lie in it.

Steadying herself, Sasha produced a smile. "Thank you. I apologize for the unannounced visit. I was hoping for a few minutes with Mrs. Holloway." Sasha leaned to the left and peered past him into the cavernous foyer beyond. "Is she home?"

"She sure is. Come on in." The long fingers of one hand wrapped around her arm and ushered her across the threshold. "Gran and I have dinner together every Sunday. We were just about to sit down at the table. We'd be thrilled to have you join us. There's always plenty to eat."

Sasha dug in her heels, stopping their forward momentum. "I couldn't possibly impose." Good grief, she had forgotten how early people had dinner around here. It wasn't even six o'clock.

"Nonsense. It's no imposition."

Before she could react to the statement, he'd taken her by the arm again and was guiding her through the house. Mrs. Holloway was beaming when they entered the dining room.

"Sassy, how sweet of you to come to dinner."

Branch pulled out a chair at the table and ushered Sasha into it. She managed a "Thank you." Then she propped a smile into place for the elderly woman across the table while Branch laid a setting for her. "It wasn't my intent to intrude. I came by to speak with you about—"

"Say grace, Branch," his grandmother ordered. "This girl needs to eat. She's as thin as a rail."

"Yes, ma'am." Branch shot Sasha a wink before sitting then bowing his head.

After the shortest dinner blessing she'd ever heard, he announced "Amen" and picked up the bowl of potatoes and passed it her way. "If you need anything at all while you're in town, you let me know. I'm sure you have your hands full."

"The hard part's over," Arlene insisted before Sasha could respond to Branch's offer. "The rest is as easy or as difficult as you choose to make it."

Funny, the older woman was far more right than she likely knew. "I appreciate the offer, Branch," Sasha said, her voice steadier than she'd hoped for. "My grandmother was very organized. She left specific instructions for everything."

Sasha nibbled at the food on her plate in an effort to appease her host and hostess. She listened avidly to their chatter about who had done what and the excitement of last month's organized crime case. Branch was still fielding offers for top assignments across the country but Arlene was hoping he would stay in Winchester.

Coffee had been poured and dessert served before Sasha had the opportunity to speak openly to Mrs. Holloway. Branch had excused himself to take a work call. Sasha wasn't sure how much time she had, so she went straight to the point.

"Mrs. Holloway, did my grandmother ever mention any second thoughts as to what happened to my parents? Did she feel satisfied with the police reports?"

Arlene stared at her for a long moment...long enough for Sasha to fear she'd shocked the poor woman.

"You received the note I had delivered."

Sasha nodded. "I did. I was quite surprised. You've never mentioned anything before."

"Your grandmother wanted the past left in the past. I felt her decision was a mistake but I held my tongue until today. Now it's time for the truth to come out, so long as you understand there will be consequences."

Sasha studied the older woman's face for some indication of exactly what she meant. "Certainly, I understand. I want the truth and I've always felt as if the truth was swept under a rug all those years ago."

There, she'd said it. It was past time she stopped pretending the truth didn't matter. It wouldn't bring her parents back but perhaps it would right a terrible wrong.

Arlene continued to stare at her, her blue eyes faded to a pale gray beneath the thick lenses of her glasses. "Your grandmother never wanted you to pick at that ugliness. Are you sure you want to go against her wishes? She's scarcely cold in her grave."

Flustered and frustrated, Sasha held her ground.

"Mrs. Holloway, with all due respect, you are the one who contacted me."

"I only made the offer—this is your journey to take."

Grappling for patience, Sasha asked, "Do you or don't you know what really happened?"

Arlene reached for her iced tea glass, took a long swallow. "I'm not sure anyone knows for certain but with the proper guidance I'm certain you could uncover the whole story."

"I'm thinking of hiring a private detective," Sasha confessed.

"A private detective?"

Branch's deep voice shook her. Sasha's attention swung to him. She hadn't realized he'd walked into the room. When she found her voice, she said, "Yes."

He pulled out his chair and dropped back into it, automatically reaching for his coffee. "Why do you need a PI?"

"She wants to know what really happened to her parents," Arlene explained. "She doesn't believe the police reports any more than I do."

Sasha cringed, as much at Branch's look of surprise as at Mrs. Holloway's words. "It's not that I don't believe the reports—I'm just not certain the investigation was as thorough as it could have been."

Branch nodded slowly. "I'm confident the investigators attempted to be thorough. Sometimes it's a matter of a failure on the part of the investigator and sometimes it's just a lack of communication. You were really young when your parents died—I can see how you would have questions now."

Sasha reminded herself to breathe. "I think you've nailed my feelings on the matter." She considered pointing out that she hadn't just shown up at his door with these questions. His grandmother had sent her a note. But she decided against that route for now. She had a feeling his grandmother had set them up for precisely this result. Sasha cleared her throat and pushed on. "With my grandmother's passing it feels like I need to settle my own affairs as well as hers. I would like to put the past to rest, I suppose."

"You can help with that, can't you, Branch?" Arlene suggested. "You're on vacation. What else have you got to do?"

He smiled patiently at his grandmother but the gesture didn't quite reach his eyes.

"No." Sasha shook her head. "I don't want to bother anyone. This is really something I need to do on my own. It's very personal."

His gaze rested on hers. "Gran's right. I'm on a long-overdue vacation and I don't have a lot planned. I can help you look into the case—if you feel comfortable with me digging around in your personal business."

If he'd said her hair was on fire she wouldn't have been more startled. Anticipation seared through her. Branch was a lawman. He would know how to conduct an investigation—that much was true. He would be able to spot the holes in the decades-old investigation. She could trust him. He would be thorough. His assistance would be invaluable.

What on earth was she saying?

She couldn't spend that kind of time with the man. There was too big a risk that he would discover her secret. Or that those old feelings that still stirred when she thought of him would be ignited all over again.

Either possibility was a chance she could not take.

"Perfect," Arlene announced. "I've always wanted to know what really happened. Out of respect for Vi, I kept my questions to myself. She never wanted to talk about it. I'm certain she was afraid of the consequences."

This was one aspect of the past Sasha had not considered. She knew in her heart that someone else was involved in the deaths of her parents. The fact that no one else seemed to feel that way and that her grandmother had been so opposed had prevented Sasha from pushing the theory over the years. But Arlene was right. If someone else was involved there would be consequences. That person or persons would want to keep the truth hidden as desperately as Sasha wanted to reveal it. Just another reason to be grateful she hadn't brought her daughter back to Winchester.

Finding the truth might be more dangerous than she had anticipated.

"When would you like to begin?"

Branch's deep voice drew her attention from the disturbing thoughts. *Breathe.* "I was hoping to start immediately." She blinked, realized it was Sunday evening only hours after her grandmother's funeral. "Tomorrow, I suppose."

He nodded. "I have a lunch meeting in Nashville tomorrow, but I can pick up the file and meet with you first."

"I would genuinely appreciate it." Anticipation lit inside her. This was really happening. "I can work with your schedule."

"I'll call Billy and let him know I'm picking up the file and we'll go from there."

Billy Brannigan was the Winchester chief of police. Sasha nodded. "Sounds good."

She thanked Mrs. Holloway for dinner and made her excuses for heading home without finishing her dessert. She wanted to spend some time going through papers and mementos at her grandmother's. Primarily, she wanted to put some distance between her and her teenage idol. Except just when she thought she was in the clear, Branch insisted on walking her out.

When they reached her car he opened the door for her and smiled; his expression looked a little sad. "I'm sure sorry about the circumstances," he offered, "but it's good to see you, Sasha. It's been a long time."

She wondered if he ever noticed that she carefully avoided him whenever she came home for a visit. Probably not. He was a busy man. She likely rarely crossed his mind, if at all. All these years, she had brought her daughter three times each year to see her g'ma and she had somehow avoided ever bumping into Branch. It was a miracle really in a town this small. And yet somehow she'd managed.

Doubt regarding the intelligence of this plan to investigate the past nudged her again. She at times second-guessed her decision about keeping Brianne a secret. But it was too late to undo that now.

All the more reason this was a really bad idea.

"It has been a while." She moved around the door, using it as a shield between them. "I'm usually only here for a couple of days when I visit. Between G'ma and Rey, I hardly see anyone else."

He nodded. "I hear you have a daughter."

Uncertainty whooshed through her like the flames from a roaring fire catching on dry kindling. She managed a laugh. "We really are behind. The daughter came into the picture ages ago."

He chuckled. "I didn't know you'd gotten married."

Her nerves jangled. "No wedding. The relationship was over before it began."

Before he could ask anything else, she threw out a few questions of her own. "What about you? Wife? Kids?"

The answer to both was no, of course. The idea that she knew this was intensely sad.

"No and no."

"Well, that's a shame, Branch. You don't know what you're missing. My daughter is amazing and brilliant. Being a parent is the best thing that ever happened to me."

Had she really just said that? Her heart swelled

into her throat. Obviously she needed to go home. Today had been overwhelming and she was clearly not thinking straight.

"It's hard to be a parent without finding the right partner first." He winked at her. "I'm beginning to think I let the only one for me get away a long time ago."

The warmth that gushed through her was at once exhilarating and terrifying. "I'll see you tomorrow." Sasha dropped behind the wheel and closed the door before Branch could say anything else.

He watched as she backed from the drive and drove away.

Branch Holloway had always been incredibly charming. He hadn't meant what he said the way it sounded—the way her mind and body took it. Sasha was certain on that one. Being kind was one of his most well-known traits. It was as natural as breathing for him.

He hadn't actually meant that she had stolen his heart and ruined him for anyone else. They'd had a one-night stand after years of her pining after him.

End of story.

At least, for Branch, it had ended there.

For Sasha, that night had only been the beginning.

Chapter Three

Chief of Police Billy Brannigan was waiting in his office for Branch's arrival. Billy had personally dropped by the archives and picked up the Lenoir file. He stood and extended his hand across his desk when Branch walked in.

"Morning, Branch. I thought you were on vacation."

Branch clasped his hand and gave it a shake. "I am. Just helping a friend."

Billy settled into his chair and tapped the file box on his desk. "This is everything we have. You looking for something in particular with this old case?"

Though Billy had been a senior when Branch made the team, they'd spent one year on the high school football team together. They'd been friends and colleagues most of the time since. Billy was a good man. He'd spent his life giving back to the community. Branch respected him, trusted him. He saw no reason to beat around the bush on the subject.

"You're aware Mrs. Simmons just passed away." Branch had spotted him at the funeral.

Billy nodded. "Viola was one of the people who insisted I step into the position of chief of police. She and about a half a dozen descendants from the town founders showed up at my door and practically demanded that I take the mayor up on his offer. Until the end of her life she still attended every single city council meeting."

"She'll be missed," Branch agreed. "You remember her granddaughter Sasha."

It wasn't really a question. Even those too young or old to remember Sasha Lenoir from when her parents died, most everyone had heard about how she worked with some of the biggest celebrities in the country. Sasha had set the gold standard for turning around a media crisis.

"I spoke to her for a moment at visitation on Saturday afternoon."

"She wants to go over the case, mostly to put that part of her past to bed once and for all. There are a lot of questions in her mind about those days. I'm hoping I can help her clear those up. She mentioned hiring a PI, but since I have some time on my hands I thought I'd save her the trouble, see if we can't find the answers."

Billy nodded. "Understandable. She was just a kid when it happened. I'm sure she has questions she wasn't mature enough to ask at the time."

"From what I gather, her grandmother didn't want her looking back, so they never talked about what happened. Now that she's gone, Sasha feels it's time to open that door."

"I'm entrusting the case file to you," the chief reminded him. "All I ask is that you keep me advised of anything you find contrary to the investigation's final conclusions and return these files intact to me when you're finished."

As chief, of course he wanted to be kept advised and aware of any red flags. Any contrary conclusions reflected on his department. "Understood." Branch got to his feet and reached for the box.

"Look forward to your insights."

Branch exited city hall and loaded the box into the back seat of his truck. It was still fairly early, only eight thirty. He imagined Sasha was still operating on Eastern time. Since he didn't have her number he couldn't shoot her a text before showing up. He'd just have to take his chances.

When he reached the Simmons house, Sasha was sitting on the front porch. Like a number of other homes in Winchester's historic downtown, the Simmons home wasn't far from anything. On the other hand, the house where Sasha had grown up—where her parents died—was outside Winchester proper, deep in the woods on the family farm. His grandmother had often commented that she didn't know why they hadn't sold that place rather than allow it to sit empty and falling into disrepair. Maybe it had been too painful to make a decision.

He grabbed the case file box and headed for the porch.

"Good morning. Would you like coffee?" She gestured to a porcelain pot waiting on a tray. "I have blueberry scones. I made them this morning."

"You've been busy." He placed the box onto a chair and settled into the one next to it.

"I'm not the only one." She poured his coffee and passed the delicate cup to him. She placed a scone on a dessert plate and handed it along next. The china was covered in pink roses and looked far too fragile for a guy like him to handle.

"Thank you, ma'am." He felt kind of foolish drinking from the fancy little cup but the scone was far tastier than he'd expected. "This is not bad, Sassy."

She lifted her eyebrows at him and he winced. "My apologies. I guess I had an awkward flashback."

Sasha laughed. "Forgiven. But just this once."

"Whew. I was worried," he teased. "I remember you socking Randy Gaines in the nose. Bled like a stuck hog."

Her hand went to her mouth to cover a smile. "I always felt bad about punching him—not at that precise moment. After I'd had time to cool off. Eventually I apologized to him. I think it was like ten years later at our first class reunion."

She looked away and silence expanded between them for the next minute or so. It didn't take a crystal ball to comprehend that she was thinking the same thing he was. They'd had sex in his truck the night of her five-year reunion. Heat boiled up around his collar. He hadn't exactly shown a lot of finesse. Since that night he had wished a hundred times for a do-over. His gut clenched at the thought. Memories of how she'd felt in his arms, the soft sounds she'd made, the way her skin had smelled, echoed through him and his body tightened with lust.

"So, have you had a look yet?" She nodded toward the box, careful to avoid eye contact.

He polished off the last bite of his scone. "No, ma'am. I waited so we could do it together."

Their gazes locked and that same lust he'd experienced a moment ago flared again. She looked away. He reached for the box. He should get his act together. She'd just lost her grandmother and she was vulnerable. The last thing he wanted was her picking up on his crazy needs.

"Let's see what we've got."

While he removed the stacks from the box, she gathered their dishes and set them on the tray. Then she disappeared into the house. By the time she returned with glasses of ice water, he'd arranged the files in chronological and workable stacks.

"So what we have here—" he opened the first folder "—are the investigator's reports, the coroner's report, crime scene photos and the medical examiner's report." He studied Sasha for a moment. He wondered if she realized how difficult this was going to be. She had the prettiest green eyes and he loved all those soft curls that fell over her face and shoulders. She was a beautiful woman. He blinked, reminded himself to stay focused. "Are you sure you want to see all the grisly details?"

She stared at him, her eyes hot with determination. "I was there, Branch. I saw everything that night. Heard my mother's screams and my father's pleas."

He nodded. "All right, then." He opened the folder and spread the photos across the table. "Your mother was lying on the living room floor. She'd been shot twice in the chest." He read the description of her father's injuries. "Your father took—"

"One shot to the head. He was dead before he fell onto the sofa. Blood was everywhere." Her voice was hollow, distant. "I had to stand on the fireplace hearth to avoid the blood."

His chest ached at the image of her as a little girl, the pigtails he recalled so vividly and those big green eyes, standing alone and surrounded by a sea of red pouring from her mother's lifeless body. "There was no indication of forced entry. The responding officers had to break down the door to get inside."

Sasha stared at the photos. "I tried to wake them up, but I couldn't. Then I called 911. But I was afraid to unlock the door when they pounded and called out to me. I'm sure I was in shock."

Her voice had gone small, like the child she had been when the tragedy happened. The urge to take her hand and remind her that she was safe now tugged at his gut.

"How about we go over the reports and you tell me if you recall anything differently than the way it was documented."

She nodded and took the pages he offered. While she read over the reports, he studied the ME's report to see if either victim showed any indication whatsoever of a struggle. The ME noted wisps of Alexandra's hair having been torn out. So he—presumably her husband—held her by the hair rather than by the wrist or arm. No scratches or bruises on either victim. No alcohol or drugs found in her mother; her father had been drinking fairly heavily. The evidence reports showed a number of unidentified fingerprints found in the house. Not unusual. People had visitors. Visitors left prints. That alone didn't mean anyone besides the family or close friends had been in the house that night or any other.

Sasha laid the investigator's final report aside and took a breath.

"Thoughts?" He waited, gave her time to collect herself. This was hard. This was exactly, he imagined, why or at least part of the reason her grandmother had never wanted to take this journey.

"That night and then again about a week after… *that night*, I told my grandmother I'd heard another voice, maybe two in the house besides my parents'. She took me to see Chief Holcomb but there's nothing in the report about my statement."

"It's possible—" Branch hoped to convey this without being too blunt "—the chief didn't feel your statement was reliable enough to enter into evidence, particularly if it was days later."

She made a face that spoke of her frustration and no small amount of anger. "I suspected that was the case. I remember Chief Holcomb suggesting that I'd dreamed about that night and my imagination had added the voices in an attempt to divert guilt from my father. He urged my grandmother to take me for counseling and she did, but those sessions didn't change what I remembered."

Branch could see how Holcomb might have come to that conclusion. For an officer of the law, logic had to be first and foremost when looking at an emotional situation. Anyone could imagine the horror and pain involved with an event like murder, but that empathy could not dictate how an investigator tackled a case.

"Denial is a powerful emotion. It's possible what Chief Holcomb suggested was exactly what happened."

She stared at him for a long moment before shaking her head. "That's not what happened. I know what I heard. I was simply too traumatized at first to explain my impressions. I've lived with this for a long time, Branch. I know what I heard. Those voices have played in my thoughts and in my dreams for twenty-seven years."

"All right, then. Let's talk about the voices." Was it possible someone else was involved? Absolutely, and if he found even a speck of evidence to support that theory, he was going the distance with it. He shuffled the crime scene photos together and placed them back into the folder. There was no need to leave those gruesome images lying in front of her. "Let's talk about the voice or voices. What exactly did you hear?"

"I heard a voice and it wasn't my father's."

"And it wasn't your mother?"

"No. It was a male voice. Deep, really deep—

and mean. I remember shaking when I heard it even though I didn't understand the words. Then I heard my mother crying and my dad pleading with someone to let her go. He kept saying *Please don't do this. Just let her go.*"

Her voice trembled with the last. "At what point did you hear the second unidentified voice?"

"When my mother started to scream, I heard another male voice. This one wasn't as deep. It sounded like he said *There's another way we can do this.* It's possible, I guess, that it was the same man, but I believe it was someone different from the first voice I heard."

Branch braced his arms on the table and considered her recounting. "Where exactly were you in the house?"

This was the point in the conversation when she shrank down in her chair, her shoulders visibly slumped, her eyes reflecting the remembered horror. "I was hiding under the stairs. When Mom and Dad argued I always hid in the closet under the stairs."

This would explain why she hadn't actually witnessed what happened. "After the gunshots, how long did you stay under the stairs?"

She shook her head. "I don't know. Minutes. An hour. Until it had been quiet for a really long time. I was too afraid to move."

Branch hesitated but then asked, "So there were sounds after the gunshots?"

She blinked. "Yes." She paused as if she'd only just considered that idea. "There were sounds. Footsteps." Her brow furrowed in concentration. "A door opened and then closed."

Branch found himself leaning forward. Every instinct he possessed told him she was telling the truth or at least what she believed to be the truth. "Were the footsteps heavy or light, a shuffle or more like a march or big steps?"

"Heavy, like the person walking was big."

"What about the door? Did he use the front door or did he exit through the back of the house?" If he remembered correctly, the staircase in the old Lenoir house was very near the front door.

"Not the front door. Farther away." She cocked her head as if trying to remember. "It must have been the back door." She suddenly nodded, the movement adamant. "Definitely the back door because I heard the squeak of the screen door, too. There was no screen door on the front."

"What happened after that?" It was important that he didn't lead her in a particular direction. Just a nudge from time to time to keep her going.

"I opened the closet door a little to try to see." She moistened her lips.

He watched, wished he hadn't. More of that foolish lust had his fingers tightening into fists.

"I didn't hear any more sounds and I couldn't see anyone, so I crawled out of the closet. I called for my mom and dad." She shook her head. "They didn't answer. So I got up and started to look for them. That's when I saw the blood." Her eyes grew bright with emotion. "I tried to wake her up. Got blood on my dress and shoes." She shuddered. "I ran to the sofa—to my dad—but there was a sizable chunk of his skull missing. I don't know how I remembered to grab the phone from the end table, but I did. I ran to the hearth and that's where I stayed until help came."

"Let's talk about what was happening in the days prior to that night." He needed to pull her away from that ugly scene. He would be talking to Holcomb about her statement. Her recounting certainly seemed credible to him. But she was an adult now. She'd had years to refine her memory. "Your parents were arguing, you said. Was the argument any more serious than usual?"

"My father had lost his job. Mother accused him of drinking too much. I think that's why he was fired. She was tired and angry. And under a lot of pressure at her job."

"Your mother worked at the municipal office."

"She was a supervisor at building inspections. The job came with a lot of stress."

He knew most of this because he'd grown up right here in Winchester with Sasha. The more they talked, the more he remembered. Looking at those photos of Sasha as a kid, a terrified, emotionally traumatized kid, tore him apart.

"I'll speak to Luther Holcomb. See if they had any leads relating to any other scenarios. Anyone who had it in for your dad or your mom."

She sat up straighter then. "Does that mean you believe me? You don't think I imagined the voices and the…?" She waved her hand in the air. "The other stuff?"

"I believe—" he chose his words carefully "—there was more to what happened than what we're finding in the reports."

"So what do we do now?"

"Now we start at the beginning of when any trouble began and we work our way up to that night. We put together the pieces we find until we discover the parts no one else has found before. We turn over every rock, we shake every tree and then we do it again until we unearth anything we didn't know before."

"But it's been so long." She pressed her fingers to her lips. "Do you think we can find the truth? Will anyone else remember?"

If Sasha's father did not murder his wife and then shoot himself, that meant someone else did. Branch could guarantee that person remembered what happened, and if Sasha's recall of the voices was accurate, at least one other person would remember, too.

"I don't know how successful we'll be but we can try."

She nodded, stood abruptly. "Thank you for agreeing to help me. You said you have a meeting in Nashville. I don't want to keep you."

Branch pushed to his feet, picked up his hat. "I'll call you as soon as I get back."

"I'll keep digging through all those reports and see what I can find."

He gave her a nod and she walked him down the

steps, then waved as he crossed the yard to his truck. Whatever truth there was to find, he would help her find it.

He just hoped the truth turned out to be what she wanted to find.

Chapter Four

Sasha stood on the sidewalk surrounded by overgrown shrubs and knee-deep grass. It all seemed so small now or maybe it was only that the woods were swallowing up the yard and the house, ruthlessly invading all within its path. White paint once gleamed from the wood siding; now it was chipped and curled away like the skin slithering from a snake. Green moss had taken up residence on the gray roof. The house looked old and tired, broken-down.

This was the first time Sasha had set foot on the property since she was nine years old. Her fingers tightened on the key she had dug from a drawer in the mudroom. After Branch had left she'd gone up to her old room and dug out a pair of boots to go with her jeans. She'd added a sweater over her blouse and buttoned it to the throat. She'd started to bring a flashlight but then she'd remembered that the electricity and the water remained on for insurance purposes. Her grandmother had arranged for any necessary expenses related to the property to be drafted directly from her bank account. Beyond that step, she had washed her hands of the property.

Weeds poked through the cracks of the sidewalk and steps. Memories of drawing with chalk and playing hopscotch sifted through her mind. She climbed the steps and crossed the porch, boards gray with age creaking beneath her weight. Unlocking the door took some doing. The lock probably needed oiling. After a couple of minutes of frustrated twisting and turning, the tumblers gave way and the lock turned.

Darkness and dust motes greeted her beyond the threshold. A memory of swiping the switch next to the door prodded her to slide her hand across the wall. An overhead light came on.

For a long time Sasha stood staring at the narrow entry hall. It wasn't very large, perhaps seven by nine. Dust was thick on the wood floor and the wool rug that might be blue or gray. Some sort of pattern attempted to emerge beyond the layer of dust but failed miserably. Cobwebs draped across the ceiling, making a path over the chandelier with its two bulbs out of six struggling to light the space. A table sat against the wall, a set of keys amid the layer of dust there. Above it a mirror hung on the wall, the glass like the windows, heavy with years of buildup.

Deep in her chest, her heart hammered as if she'd run miles and miles.

The worst was the smell. Decades of mustiness with an underlying hint of copper. The stillness gave the sense of a lack of air. It was hard to breathe. Sasha drew in a deep breath that seemed to dissipate before it reached her lungs. To the right was a small parlor that her mother had used as a home office and straight ahead was the living room, a hall, dining room and the kitchen and a bathroom. The bedrooms and another bathroom were upstairs.

If she kept going, only a few more steps, she would enter the living room. Someone had cleaned up the bloody mess. She'd heard her grandmother discussing it a few weeks after that night. Friends or neighbors had rid the place of all indications of the bad thing that had happened.

Bad thing.

A very bad thing had happened in this house. Sasha forced one foot in front of the other. As she entered the parlor, voices vibrated in her mind. Her mother crying…her father pleading…the other voices growling with such menace. Sasha stood very still; she stared at the staircase and the door that was hidden until you walked beyond the newel post. She'd hidden there so many times.

Her heart pounding harder and harder, she continued on, along the hall and into the kitchen, turning on lights as she went. It looked exactly the same save for the cobwebs and dust. The teakettle still sat on the stove, the red-and-white-checked mitt hung from a drawer pull nearby.

You'll be late for school.

Her mother always worried that Sasha would be late for school. Or that she wouldn't finish her homework or her breakfast.

The newspaper from their final morning in the

house lay on the kitchen table where her father had left it.

She stared at the headlines from that date. Man Is Killed by Lightning Strike while Working on Barn Roof. New Hospital Construction Is Moving Forward.

Sasha walked through the dining room on her way back to the living room. This time she forced herself to take a closer look. The spot on the floor in the center of the room where her mother had fallen. The rug that had once been there had been taken away. The sofa was gone, as well. Her father's blood and brain matter had been sprayed over the upholstery. All that remained were two chairs with a table between them. The princess-style phone still sat on the table. Sasha had dragged its long cord over to the hearth that night to escape the reach of her mother's blood flowing across the floor.

Please don't do this. Just let her go!

Sasha blinked away the voices and moved toward the stairs. The runner was coated in dust. The steps creaked as she climbed upward. Her fingers trailed along the wooden banister the same way she'd done as a child. Her father had grown up in this house. His grandfather had built it. Her father had been a good man. Never raised his voice. Was always a gentleman with her or her mother. No one could understand what happened to his temperament. Surely losing his job had not turned him into a killer.

No. Sasha shook off the notion. Someone else had been in the house. Her father had not done this and it was time she proved it and cleared his name. Both he and her mother deserved justice.

Someone had murdered them. Sasha was certain of it.

Two doors on the right were the guest room and a bathroom; on the left was her room and then that of her parents. She walked through her parents' room first. The bed was made. Sasha crouched down and checked underneath the bed skirt on her father's side. His old high school baseball bat was still there. He had called it his security system. Anyone broke into their house, the security system was going off.

Sasha stood and moved to the other side of the bed. Her mother's heels lay next to the closet door where she'd come home that evening and shed her work attire. She always stripped off the suit and pulled on jeans and a tee or a sweater. Her father wore jeans and work boots all the time. His work as a construction superintendent rarely required a shirt and tie. They had been so different and yet so suited for each other.

At least until the last few weeks of their lives. Things had been tense. Very tense.

Even as a child Sasha had sensed the extreme tension.

Her mother's pearls lay across a small mirror on the dresser. Sasha fingered the necklace. Alexandra Lenoir had worn those pearls every Monday and Friday. She had laughed and said she wanted to feel special on Mondays and she wanted to be ready to celebrate on Fridays. The pearls were a gift to her mother from her father, Sasha's grandfather, when her mother was sixteen, the year before he died. They were the only piece of jewelry her grandmother hadn't had the heart to remove from the house. She'd wanted the pearls to stay exactly where her daughter left them.

Sasha stared at her reflection in the mirror standing above the dresser. Other than the lightness of her skin and the green eyes, she looked exactly like her mother. Same features and profile. Her mother had been a very beautiful woman.

She turned away from her reflection and walked out of the room and into the one that had belonged to her as a child. Her white canopy bed with its pink lace and mound of stuffed animals was heavy with dust. Posters of cartoon characters and butterflies dotted the walls. Her favorite doll was at her grandmother's. It was the only item Sasha had wanted to take with her.

Her grandmother had bought her an entire new wardrobe so she wouldn't have to be reminded of her former life if she didn't want to be. Looking back, she and her grandmother had both been in denial. They had looked forward, never once looking back, and pretended the bad thing had not happened. It was easier that way. They became a family unit.

No looking back. No looking back.

Sasha sat down on her bed and allowed her surroundings to soak in. The lavender walls and the hair bows on the dresser. Her mother had loved brushing and braiding Sasha's hair. Giggles and the sound of the brush stroking through her hair whispered through her mind.

Life had been good here all the way up until it wasn't. She should have looked back, should have cherished the memories rather than trying to forget them.

But her grandmother had wanted to protect her. How do you protect a child? You insulate her from danger, from harm.

The denial, the memories that refused to stay buried had haunted her. It was time to unearth them and learn the truth.

Sasha descended the stairs and rounded the newel post. She grasped the knob of the closet door and gave it a twist, opening the door. The closet looked even smaller now. Maybe two feet by three. The only thing inside the closet was dust. There had been raincoats as she recalled. She could only assume they had been moved during the processing of the house for evidence. After all, she'd been hiding in the closet.

Sasha stepped into the closet and pulled the door closed, pitching the tiny space into darkness. She squatted down, hugged her knees and allowed her bottom to slide down to the floor. Then she closed her eyes.

You had a chance to save yourself...

Her eyes shot open as the voice echoed through her. It was the man's voice—the one with the deep, menacing voice.

Please don't do this. Just let her go.

Gunshots erupted in the darkness.

Sasha bolted upward and pushed out of the cramped space.

She couldn't breathe.

She ran out of the house and across the porch, down the steps. *Deep breaths. Slow it down.*

Perspiration covered her skin.

She focused on her breathing, told herself over and over to calm down.

A panic attack had not managed to get the drop on her in ages. Not since she was a teenager.

She braced her hands on her hips and breathed. Her heart rate began to slow. Still the dense woods seemed to close in on her.

If you go down to the woods today...you'd better not go alone.

The old nursery rhyme murmured through her. She'd loved exploring the woods around their home when she was a kid, but after that night she had been terrified of the woods. She'd gone camping once with a friend and her family and suffered her first panic attack that night in the woods.

Pulling herself together, Sasha walked back into the house and turned out the lights and locked the door. She climbed into her car and backed away, the trees closing in on the place sticking in her mind as she drove back into town.

She had a feeling if she didn't find the truth soon it would vanish forever.

TAREK MARTIN STILL lived in the same house he'd bought when he and his wife married, the same summer Sasha's mother and father had married. The two couples had their daughters within two years of each other and both men worked at Kimble & Douglas, K&D, the largest construction firm in a tri-county area. Sasha's father, Brandon, had often joked that imitation was the purest form of flattery and that Tarek had been flattering him for years.

Mr. Martin was one of the few people who had stood by her father during the investigation. He had insisted that Brandon Lenoir would never hurt his wife. His insistence hadn't changed the coroner's report.

Burt Johnston, the same man who was county coroner now, had concluded murder-suicide, and the medical examiner's autopsy, though inconclusive, had not disagreed.

Sasha had almost called Mr. Martin before driving to his home, but she'd decided that surprise would be a handy element under the circumstances. Never allow one's adversary an advantage. An announcement that the daughter of your former best friend was going to pay you a visit after more than two decades was turning over a fairly large advantage.

She opened the screen door, it squeaked and she knocked on the door. A television blasted the laughter and cheers of a game show. When she knocked a second time a dog barked. Sounded like a small breed. Sasha allowed the screen door to close between her and the wood door just in case the dog made a dive for the stranger doing all the knocking.

The knob twisted and the door opened. The voice

of the talk show host blared out around the big man filling the door frame. Tarek Martin was considerably heavier than he'd been the last time Sasha saw him and his hair was gray through and through; his face looked significantly craggier but she easily recognized him.

His breath caught and he hissed it out between his teeth. "Sassy Lenoir, as I live and breathe."

She opted not to call him on the use of her nickname. "Mr. Martin, how are you, sir?"

"Well, I'm fine." He reached to push the screen door open. "Come on in here, little girl." He hollered over his shoulder, "Edie, come see who's here."

The little white dog hopped around his feet, yapping madly.

Sasha dared to step inside, expecting a snip at her heels. But the little dog just continued to bounce and bark.

A woman, obviously his wife, wandered into the living room, drying her hands on her apron. "I swear, you look just like your mama, honey."

Sasha didn't remember Edie Martin. Her voice was vaguely familiar but her face drew a blank. "Thank you."

The older woman's mouth formed an O. "I am so sorry about your grandmother. We came to the funeral but we didn't get a chance to talk to you. It was so crowded."

Sasha nodded. "G'ma had a lot of friends."

"She sure did," Mr. Martin said. "Come on in here

and sit down. Can we get you something to drink? Coffee or tea?"

Sasha shook her head. "No, thank you. I just wanted to ask you a few questions if you have a moment."

"Course." He gestured to the sofa as he and his wife claimed the chairs they obviously preferred.

"I suppose you're busy taking care of your grandmother's affairs?" Mrs. Martin commented.

"Yes, ma'am. There's lots to do."

Mr. Martin grinned. "You sure enough pulled that pop star out of the fire last month."

Sasha smiled, her first real one of the day. "Yes, I did." The pop star in question had really blown his image on social media recently. Sasha had turned the situation around for him and set him on a better track. It was up to him now to stay the course.

"Your grandmother was so proud of you. She was always talking about you everywhere she went."

"I appreciate you sharing that with me."

Mr. Martin's craggy face scrunched up. "You said you had some questions. You know we're happy to help any way we can."

Sasha squared her shoulders. "When my parents died, Mr. Martin, you were the one person who stood up for my father. You insisted he would never have done such a thing."

Mr. Martin shook his head firmly from side to side. "I stand by those words still. There is no way Brandon would have hurt Alexandra. No way in the world."

"No way," his wife echoed. "They were having some problems with him getting fired and all, but they loved each other. He wouldn't have hurt a fly, much less his sweet wife."

Sasha blinked back the tears that threatened. "I tried to tell everyone that myself, but no one listened." She swallowed the lump in her throat and pushed on. "Can you think of any reason anyone would have wanted to hurt either of my parents?"

"You see," Mr. Martin said, "that's the thing. Everybody loved those two. I mean you had your jerk who made some remark about the fact that your mama was black and your daddy was white, but that was rare. I honestly can't remember more than one occasion that it happened and that was years before... that night."

"Why was my father fired? The reports say he was drinking on the job."

He scoffed. "That's another thing that was stretched out of proportion. Yes, he'd had a couple of drinks, but he was not falling-down drunk. Your daddy wasn't much of a drinker in the first place. The real problem is he crossed the wrong person and that person was looking for a way to be rid of him."

"Who did he cross?"

"Dennis Polk, the crew chief at our site. Dennis didn't like your daddy. To tell you the truth, I think he had a thing for your mama and didn't like the man she chose. I think I heard something about her dating Dennis back in high school but that's pure hearsay."

"Whether she did or not—" Mrs. Martin took

over from there "—your mama had no use for the man. He had it in for your daddy, and as soon as he got that promotion to crew chief, he found a way to get him in trouble." She shook her head. "But they were working that situation out. Your mama had a good job that included a health insurance plan. They had the house they'd inherited. There were no real money issues. I think your daddy just felt like he wasn't pulling his weight those last few weeks and that caused tension."

Words echoed through Sasha. Her parents arguing over his need to find work and to stop moping around. She pushed the memories away. "Is it possible Mr. Polk may have wanted to hurt my parents?"

Mr. Martin moved his hands back and forth as if to erase the idea. "Oh, no, not in a million years. Polk was a weasel, rightly enough, but he didn't have the guts to do anything like that. He was all talk." Martin laughed. "Still is, as a matter of fact."

"There was that drug operation," Mrs. Martin said. "Brandon came across it deep in the woods behind your house in that old shack. Remember?" She directed the question to her husband.

"I sure do. We told the chief about it and he looked into it, but those knuckleheads were long gone. Drifters, I think."

"I didn't read anything about that in the reports from the investigation."

"I know it was looked into," Mr. Martin countered. "I took Chief Holcomb through those woods personally. Showed him the shack and told him the whole story same as Brandon told me."

"What about my mother?" Sasha looked from one to the other. "Did she have any enemies who might have wanted to hurt her?"

Both shook their heads. "Folks loved her. She was always so helpful with the permits and zoning issues. Anytime anyone wanted a permit to build or change something on their home, they went to Alexandra first even though she was in planning and development. She did it right and she did it fair. None of that playing favorites or making things more difficult than necessary."

"Your mama was under a lot of pressure that year," Mr. Martin said. "Her boss had a heart attack and that left only her to oversee everything going on in the county and to keep up with all the inspectors. It was a difficult time. Especially with the hospital and the big-box store going up that year. It was a real mess."

Frustration inched up Sasha's spine. These were the people closest to her parents. If they didn't know of anyone who wanted to hurt one or both, who would? "But there was no one related to her work who might have wanted to hurt her or have revenge for some action she'd taken or failed to take?"

More shaking of heads. Sasha felt her hopes deflate.

"Can you tell me where Mr. Polk lives?" She might as well talk with him, too. She had nothing to lose but time.

"Over at the Shady Pines nursing home," Mr. Martin said. "He had a stroke some years back and he can't get around too well, but he can talk. He's a little difficult to understand at times."

"I appreciate your help." Sasha reached into her handbag for a business card. She passed it to Mrs. Martin. "If you think of anything at all that you feel might be useful in my search for answers, please call me. I would really like to find the truth."

Mrs. Martin saw her to the door. Both she and her husband assured Sasha they would contact her if they recalled anything useful.

If she had to interview every single person who had known one or both of her parents, she intended to do so. Someone had to have seen or heard something.

Murder didn't happen without leaving ripples.

Chapter Five

The Shady Pines assisted living facility had been around as long as Sasha could remember. As a child her grandmother had brought her here to visit one of her teachers, Ms. Clements, who had been in a terrible accident. She had no husband or family, so she'd had to stay in this facility through her rehab. Three months later she was able to return home but she was never able to teach again. Ms. Clements had been Sasha's favorite teacher. She was the one to sit in the bathroom with her whenever she felt the need to cry that first year back at school after her parents died.

Sasha should visit her while she was in Winchester. Ms. Clements would love seeing photos of Sasha's daughter. She smiled to herself as she thought of all the things about her childhood that she needed to show her daughter…including the father her daughter didn't know.

The realization startled Sasha but there was no denying the truth.

She put her car in Park and shut off the engine. For years now she had been telling herself that she should talk to Brianne about her father. Her daughter had gone through that phase where she'd asked every other day about her father. Sasha had told her that he was a good man but that he didn't know he had a daughter. So far Brianne hadn't questioned her mother further but Sasha understood the time was coming. Her daughter was quickly going from a child to a teenager.

The truth was, how could Sasha be so intent on having the truth about her own childhood when she concealed her daughter's? She had been afraid to tell Branch. Not at first. At first she'd been certain he wouldn't be interested, so she had chosen not to tell him. Their one night together hadn't been about love or the promise of a future; it had been about need and happenstance. Neither was a good foundation for a relationship. She had told herself that Branch wouldn't want to be weighed down with fatherhood and at the time that was most likely the case.

Years later, on a visit to her grandmother, she had run into him again. He, too, was home for a visit and he had talked and talked about how exciting his work was in Chicago. He had been happy, focused singularly on his career. Again, Sasha had told herself that she had made the right decision. But then, two years ago her grandmother had shared Arlene's concerns about how lonely Branch was. He'd mentioned to Arlene that he worried that he'd waited too long to pursue a real relationship…that maybe a family wasn't in the cards for him.

Sasha had always intended to find a way to tell

him, but time had slipped away. Her grandmother had never advised her either way. She'd said Sasha would know what to do when the time came.

"I'm still waiting for that time to come, G'ma."

She climbed out of her car, draped her bag over her shoulder and headed for the assisted living center entrance. After a stop at the registration desk, she wove her way along the corridors until she found the room belonging to resident Dennis Polk. Though the facility wasn't a five-star resort, it was certainly well maintained.

Sasha knocked on the door and a surprisingly strong male voice shouted for her to come in. She opened the door and stepped inside. The room was neat and spacious. Mr. Polk sat in a chair by a large window that washed the room in sunlight. His bed was made, a patchwork quilt folded across the foot, and a small arrangement of flowers sat on the bedside table. The television was tuned to a news channel.

Mr. Polk eyed her over the top of his reading glasses for a moment. His curly dark hair had gone mostly gray now. She vaguely recalled meeting him at a company picnic once. His tall frame was far thinner and his ebony skin sagged from his chin. But his eyes were bright and alert.

"Mr. Polk, I'm—"

"I know who you are." His words were a little rough and clipped but easy enough to understand. He closed his book and laid it on the window ledge. "You're Alexandra and Brandon's girl."

She smiled and moved a little closer. "Yes, sir. I am. I'd like to ask you a few questions if you have the time."

"I have all the time in the world, young lady." He gestured to the small sofa. "Please, join me."

Sasha took the offered seat. "I don't know if you heard, but my grandmother passed away."

"I heard." He nodded to the small radio perched on the table next to his chair. "I listen to the local talk show every morning. They always announce who's married and who's passed and so forth. She was a good woman and a lucky one. Her granddaddy made a fortune on a land deal when the dam came in and he bought his wife one of those stately historic homes. They were the first folks of color to own one. Did you know that?"

Sasha nodded. "I did." Her grandmother had told her the story when Sasha was just a child but she never spoke of it again. Viola Simmons did not believe in rehashing the past. She was a firm believer in moving forward without looking back and dwelling on the things that had already occurred. All the more reason Sasha needed to find the truth—whatever it was—and move on with her life. There was no future in dwelling in the past.

"I was in love with your mama. Did you know that?" His expression was a little sheepish now.

Sasha met his gaze and asked the question burning inside her. "Is that why you got my father fired from his job?"

His eyebrows shot up. "There were folks who believed that was the reason and I have to tell you that I certainly was looking for a reason to give him his comeuppance. But no, I didn't turn him in on account of how I felt about your mother. I turned him in because he came to the job site drunk. Drunker than a skunk, I'm telling you."

Hurt speared through her. She had wanted to believe otherwise. "My father wasn't much of a drinker." This she remembered quite well, which was why she'd held out hope that the story was wrong.

"That's true and that's also why I was so surprised that he came into work at six in the morning with alcohol on his breath and staggering. I took him off to the side and asked him what was going on. He got defensive and told me it was none of my business." Polk shook his head. "I surprised myself when after all that time of looking for a reason to get him into trouble, I felt sorry for him instead. I knew something wasn't right. Brandon Lenoir wasn't a drinker."

The ache inside Sasha eased. "Did he tell you what happened?"

"He and your mother argued over something. He wouldn't say what. He just kept repeating that there was nothing he could do. He couldn't fix it and that seemed to have him awfully upset."

"Do you have any idea what he meant?"

Polk shook his head again. "I don't. I tried to talk to him, to reason with him, but he was having none of it. I told one of the other guys to take him home and I warned your daddy to sleep it off and come back the next day. I'll be damned if he didn't take a swing at me. Knocked me flat on my back but good, I'm telling you. I thought he'd broken my jaw, but lucky for me the worst damage was to my pride." He shrugged. "I didn't have a choice then. I had to fire him but I told him when he got his act together to come back and we'd work something out. The next thing I knew, he and your mama were dead."

His tone and his downcast gaze told her he felt partially responsible. "Did you ever hear any rumors about what happened? Maybe an opinion that differed from the official conclusion?"

His faded brown gaze lifted to meet hers. "I heard lots of opinions but none of them were any truer than the one the police came up with."

Her pulse rate accelerated. "So you don't believe my father killed my mother and then himself."

Polk shook his head firmly from side to side. "There is no way on God's green earth that Brandon Lenoir hurt his wife. He loved her too much. He would've done anything for her."

Sasha took a much-needed breath, hadn't realized she'd been holding it as he spoke. "Then who killed them?"

"That's the question, isn't it?" He stared out the window for a time as he spoke. "I'm pretty sure they didn't have any enemies. In a small town you hear those sorts of things. Never heard any talk like that about your folks."

Sasha hesitated. Should she tell him what she remembered hearing? Why not? Maybe it would spur some lost memory of his. "I heard at least one other person in the house that night. It was a man, perhaps two. My father pleaded with him or them to let my mother go."

Polk's gaze locked onto hers again. "Did you tell Holcomb about that?"

She nodded. "Apparently he felt my statement was too little too late. By the time I could tell someone they'd already concluded the murder-suicide scenario based on the lack of evidence for any other theory. I can't really blame the police. You said yourself my parents had no enemies. There was no evidence to support what I heard."

"It's been twenty-seven years. Digging at it won't change nothing at all. Sometimes it's just best to let sleeping dogs lie." He reached for his book and opened it, started to read once more—or pretended to.

Sasha recognized the cue. He was through talking. She retrieved a card from her bag and placed it on the table next to him. "If you think of anything else that might help, please call me."

He gave a single nod but didn't look up from his book. Sasha left his room. How could everyone be so convinced her father would never do this and yet sit back and let the whole thing go as if it made no difference?

Outside she unlocked her car and slid behind the steering wheel. The question that haunted her now echoed in her brain.

What difference will it make? Dead is dead. Her

grandmother had said those words to her once when Sasha was fifteen and demanding answers.

She started the engine, braced her hands on the steering wheel. What now? Who else should she interview? Years ago she should have demanded that her grandmother help her do this. Now the one person who had known her parents better than anyone was dead. How was she supposed to piece together this mystery without her grandmother?

Tears spilled down her cheeks. Despite her best efforts to contain the flood, Sasha surrendered. She laid her forehead against the steering wheel and let them flow. She hadn't allowed herself to cry—to really cry—since she got the call about her grandmother. She'd been too busy, too shrouded in disbelief to totally break down.

Apparently there was no holding it back any longer. She pawed through the console of the rental car looking for a tissue or a napkin, anything with which to wipe her eyes and nose. The more she searched for something to dry her tears, the harder she cried. By the time the stream had slowed, she was exhausted and weak with an odd sort of relief.

She finally found a pack of tissues in her bag. She cleaned up her face as best she could and took a long, deep breath. She would get through this. As much as she had wanted to have her grandmother around forever, that wasn't possible. But what she could keep for the rest of her life were the memories. Memories that she would pass down to her daughter.

Sasha put the car in Drive and rolled out of the

parking lot. The most important thing she could do for the memory of her family was to prove her father's innocence and to see that the person who murdered her parents was brought to justice.

If that person was still alive. Twenty-seven years was a long time. He could be dead or in prison or in a nursing home.

But, if he was alive, he had gotten away with murder for more than a quarter of a century. It was well beyond time to rectify that wrong.

THOUGH IT WAS still hours until dark, the sun had dropped behind the trees, leaving the old Lenoir home place cast in shadow. Sasha parked in front of the house and climbed out. She had her cell for all the good it would do. Cell service in the area was sketchy at best.

She unlocked the house and tucked the key into the hip pocket of her jeans. First, she walked through the downstairs and turned on lights, chasing away a portion of the creep factor. It was impossible to shake the idea that the deep, dark woods that surrounded the house appeared to be closing in a little more each year. She should probably have a service come out and clear the yards back to the original boundaries.

Upstairs she noted a few dark spots on the ceilings. The roof was deteriorating. She had to make a decision about this place soon or it was going to collapse into a heap. Her grandmother hadn't cared. She never wanted to come back here. But Sasha had cried each time she spoke of selling it. Some part of her had hoped one day she would wake up in her bed in the room she'd slept in as a child. That her parents would be gathered around the breakfast table, smiling and wishing her a good morning.

But she was not a child anymore. All the hope and wishing in the world wouldn't bring her parents back. It was time she did what needed to be done.

That would mean clearing out her parents' things as well as her childhood possessions. She felt confident there was someone she could call to donate whatever remained usable.

But first she had to determine what, if anything, she wanted to keep. Her grandmother had left most all their worldly possessions right here in this house. There were photo albums and keepsakes. The family Bible and a million other things that Sasha needed to consider before walking away.

She started with her parents' bedroom. The bedside tables were first. She went through each drawer, her mind instantly conjuring a memory connected to each object she touched. From her mother's favorite lotion to her father's wallet. She thumbed through the contents of the wallet. On the very top inside was a photo of Sasha and her mother. It was worn from being stored in his wallet but the images of their smiling faces said it all.

Happiness.

What had happened to change that?

Another thought occurred to Sasha. She glanced around the room. Where was her mother's purse? She summoned the image. White leather trimmed, a sort of tan-colored bag, some straw-like material since it was summer. The end of June.

Sasha searched the closet, looked under the bed, and then she went to the single shared bath on the second floor. No purse. Downstairs, she started with the small mudroom off the kitchen. Her mother's sweater hung on one of the hooks near the door. A windbreaker that had belonged to her father was there, too. She checked the pockets. A piece of peppermint candy was in her mother's right pocket. Beneath the sweater was her purse. Her wallet was there. Staring at the driver's license photo made her stomach hurt. The pressed powder compact, a brush and lipstick cluttered the bottom of the bag. A receipt from the local grocery store dated two days before her death.

Sasha walked through the kitchen, checked under the table and in all the cabinets, though she couldn't see her mother storing any big secrets in the cabinets. Then she moved on to the dining room and living room. She checked under tables, behind chairs and in bookcases. No surprises.

The same in the entry hall. An umbrella stood in the corner.

Her mother's office was cluttered and as dusty as the rest of the house. Framed accolade after framed accolade filled one wall. Her mother had graduated from architecture school at the top of her class. She'd spent two years in Nashville working but then she'd fallen in love with Sasha's father and she'd come home to marry him and to start a family. It wasn't until Sasha was in kindergarten that her mother took the position with the city in planning and development.

Sasha surveyed the rolls and rolls of plans on her mother's desk. There were dozens of notes in a stack next to the phone and more on the bulletin board; all appeared to be about work.

One by one she scanned the notes on the bulletin board. All were related to upcoming deadlines at work. A stack of file folders waited on one corner of the desk. Her mother had made notes on call sheets and forms attached to the folders. Most looked like copies, not originals. Sasha assumed she had a working copy at home and the originals at work. Her fingers stalled on the photos tucked under the glass on the desk. Sasha's green eyes and big smile beamed out from the one in the middle. There was another of her parents in a hug, their lips just touching. Her heart squeezed. How had two people who seemed to love each other so much and who had everything necessary for happiness ended up dead in such a violent, heinous manner?

Sasha banished the question and moved on to the drawers. She found her mother's peppermint stash. She unwrapped a piece of the red-and-white candy and popped it into her mouth. Still tasted okay. More work files and office supplies but nothing else.

A memory of her mother working late in this office flashed through Sasha's mind. Her position had been very stressful and demanding. But could it have had anything to do with her death? Sasha couldn't see how. She'd only been in the position for four years. Perhaps an outsider coming in and taking a top spot had caused some resentment. But was that enough motive for murder?

There was that woman with whom her mother had lunch occasionally. What was her name? Penny something. Sasha remembered her, mostly because she always seemed to be intense, so needy. She should find the woman and ask her about her mother's work. First, though, she had to figure out what the woman's name was. Her attention settled on the old Rolodex and she reached for it. Seemed like a good place to start looking for names.

She moved from *A* to *B* and so on, turning the wheel to the next letter. Still no Penny. Maybe she had the name wrong. Could be some other *P* name. Patty? Pricilla? Penelope?

The digital number on the phone snagged her attention. It was one of those old-fashioned phones with the built-in answering machine.

"Old as dirt." Sasha studied the device. The handset was cordless, so not entirely ancient.

A number 2 stared at her from the small window that displayed the total of stored messages on the answering machine. Sasha had no idea if the machine still worked, but the small button glowed red for answering machine on.

With nothing to lose, she pressed the play button. The first message was from the dentist's office, reminding Mrs. Lenoir that her daughter Sasha had an appointment the next day.

That appointment hadn't taken place for another month.

Another voice echoed in the room. The sound quality was a little scratchy but it was certainly clear enough to understand.

We need to talk, Alex. Call me as soon as you can. It's important.

The date-and-time stamp indicated the message had been left the afternoon of the day before her parents died.

Was this the woman who had been her mother's friend? Penny or Patty or whatever?

It's important.

Maybe this woman had the answers Sasha needed.

All she had to do was figure out who her mom's friend was and then find her…assuming she was still alive. And that she was the woman who had left that message.

With nearly three decades having elapsed, anything could have happened.

Chapter Six

It was almost dark by the time Branch reached the Winchester city limits. He had tried to call Sasha since he passed the Tullahoma exit but she hadn't been answering. He just kept getting her voice mail. Since he had promised to catch up with her as soon as he was back in town, he headed to her grandmother's house.

He'd done a lot of thinking on the drive back from Nashville and none of it was about the offer he'd been made in the meeting. The promotion and the opportunities available in Nashville were a far cry from the future he could expect in Winchester and still he hesitated.

As crazy as it sounded, he had sort of grown accustomed to the slower pace in Winchester and being around family and old friends. But the Nashville offer was one he'd been hoping would come his way for a long while now. He'd been certain the trouble in Chicago early last year had set his career back at least a decade. Last month's high-profile takedown had launched his career back up to where it belonged.

As gratifying as the offer was, at the moment he couldn't keep the Lenoir case off his mind. There was more to what happened twenty-seven years ago than was in the pages of those investigation reports. Maybe it was all the years of his grandmother shaking her head and commenting about what a travesty the investigation into the case had been.

She had insisted that Brandon Lenoir would never have murdered his wife. The question was, why hadn't Viola Simmons demanded the case be reopened? She had kept quiet and allowed the police to do their job, whatever the outcome. Not once had Branch ever heard his grandmother mention Mrs. Simmons's thoughts on the matter. Maybe Mrs. Simmons believed his grandmother spoke loudly enough for both of them. But he had watched the elderly lady go after councilmen in city council meetings. He'd witnessed her speaking on behalf of the lack of opportunities for young black women in the area. When Viola Simmons believed in something, she went the distance.

Why hold back when it came to the murder of her own daughter?

It just didn't fit.

He parked in front of the Simmons home and made his way to the door. He knocked twice. No answer. No sound inside. Sasha's rental car wasn't in the driveway or on the street. She had said she would be reviewing the reports. Maybe she'd found something she wanted to follow up on. He sure wished she had kept him informed. He would have to talk to her about the need to stay in touch. Going off on her own wasn't a good idea. She could run into trouble and he'd have no idea what happened.

He called her cell again and this time it went straight to voice mail.

For the next half minute he considered what he would do if it was his history he was attempting to dissect and correct.

First, he wouldn't have screwed things up with her all those years ago. He'd been attracted to her since high school but she had completely ignored him. She'd always been busy with her friends. Always had a boyfriend hanging around. No surprise there. Sasha was the prettiest girl in school. The biggest stumbling block had been his grandmother. She had warned Branch about doing anything that might in any way take advantage of or hurt Sasha. She had been through enough, his grandmother cautioned.

And he had. He'd done exactly what his grandmother told him…until that fall Sasha showed up for a high school reunion. If she had been pretty growing up, she had become a stunningly beautiful woman. Just looking at her had taken his breath. That one night, thirteen years ago, had turned him inside out. He hadn't managed a serious relationship since. Oh, he'd had plenty of dates, but none that had gone beyond the physical. He hadn't met anyone who made him want more.

Work had consumed his life. And he had been exceedingly good at his job. Then he'd made the mistake of his life by getting involved with a witness and she'd lost her life because of his error. That wasn't entirely true. He had been cleared of wrong-doing related to her death, but deep down he would always feel that if he'd done things differently maybe he could have seen what was coming.

He would second-guess himself on that one for the rest of his life.

Clearing his head of the troubling memories, he decided to check the old Lenoir place. It was possible Sasha had decided to have a look around in the house without him. Not that he could blame her. There was no better way to put herself in the middle of the past than by going back to the scene of the crime.

The Lenoir house wasn't that far outside Winchester proper, still in the city limits but nestled deep in the woods off South Shephard and Gem. The area was densely wooded and the old place had been abandoned since Sasha's parents died. Mrs. Simmons refused to allow the property to be sold or rented, or even maintained.

Weeds had encroached on the long driveway, making it narrower. Cracked and broken asphalt aided the weed coup. He breathed a little easier when he spotted Sasha's rental car parked near the house. He had no more appointments for the next few days, which left him free to focus on this investigation. And her.

He shook his head, reminded himself that he had to look at this as a case—not as a personal venture. This was not about spending time with Sasha—well, maybe it was in part—it was about finding the truth. There was an aspect of the case he needed to find an opportunity to present to her. As much as she wanted to clear her father completely of any fault in what had happened, Branch worried that wouldn't be possible. One of the two victims, either her father or her mother, was involved on some level. People rarely got murdered in this manner—planned and executed—without some degree of involvement.

First thing, they needed to set some ground rules. Although he had no reason to believe either of them was in danger related to this exploration of the past, it was best not to take any chances. If they learned someone else was responsible for her parents' murders, that person in all probability would not want his secret revealed.

If that person was still alive.

Branch wanted to remain objective on this case but he was having a difficult time doing so. Maybe because of his grandmother's certainty, maybe simply because he wanted a different ending for Sasha.

He thought of her daughter. Was there still a connection between her and the girl's father? She hadn't mentioned a relationship with the man but it was more likely than not. After what Sasha had been through losing her parents, he felt confident she would want her daughter to have a relationship with both her parents if possible.

He walked to the door and knocked. It was quiet inside. He glanced around the overgrown yard. He would call the lawn service his mother used and have them come over and work on the property. Sasha would potentially want to put it up for sale now. He wasn't sure it would pass any sort of inspection considering the condition of the roof and the siding, but all those things could be repaired. It could be a nice place again. A little TLC would go a long way.

He reached up to knock again and the door opened. She started, stared up at him in surprise.

"You didn't answer your phone." He removed his hat, held it with both hands, mostly to keep them busy since his first instinct was to reach out and touch her.

She frowned. "The service is really bad out here. Sorry. I guess I should have sent you a text to let you know where I'd be."

"How's it going?"

"I haven't found anything earth-shattering." She shrugged. "Anyway, come in. I can't offer you any refreshments because there's nothing here."

He followed her through the entry hall and then into a room to the right. Her mother's office. Sasha went around behind the desk and sat down. She pushed a button on the phone. "Listen to this."

He listened through two messages. The first was an appointment confirmation; the second was from a female who urged Alexandra to call her. "Do you know the caller?"

She shook her head. "I tried to review the numbers on the caller ID but they're no longer available. The only reason the messages are still there is because it's one of those old answering machines with the cassette tape."

"The voice doesn't sound familiar to you?"

"It's too scratchy or low, maybe both. I know Mother had a friend, Penny or Patty. Something like that. I've been looking through her Rolodex and her notes. I haven't found a reference to a female with a name that starts with *P*."

"Rolodex? Really?"

The hint of a smile peeked beyond her obvious weariness. "Believe it or not, there are people in this world who would die protecting their Rolodex. For a businessman or woman who's been around since before contact lists and smartphones, a Rolodex is sacred."

She gave the Rolodex wheel a spin; the alphabetized cards tumbled around the wheel. "I can ask my grandmother if she remembers anyone in particular who was friends with your mom."

Sasha's gaze lit up. "That would be great. I considered calling her but I thought I'd exhaust my other options first."

"Frankly, I'm surprised the phone and the answering machine weren't taken into evidence."

"That was my first thought," she agreed. "It feels like the investigators had made up their minds and simply didn't bother looking for evidence."

He wasn't prepared to go that far just yet, but he had to admit that there was a lot that had been missed. Then again, hindsight was twenty-twenty.

"Why don't you give me a tour—if you're up to it." Branch had been here a few times growing up, but he never paid much attention to the layout of the house. He'd always been focused on the green-eyed princess who lived here.

"Sure." She pushed away from the desk and stood. "Obviously you can see this was her home office. She worked a lot of long hours and she didn't like spending so many away from Dad and me. So, she brought homework from the job nearly every day."

They moved into the living room and she walked him through the scene though he already had a good grasp from the crime scene photos. The closet where Sasha had been hiding was literally less than a dozen yards from where her parents had died. God Almighty. No child should have to go through that kind of trauma.

The kitchen and dining room were next. Branch stared out the rear windows at the gathering gloom. "Do you remember exploring those woods as a kid?"

"I do. There was an old shack. Rey and I used to use it for a playhouse. We spent hours pretending to clean and cook."

He wondered if that was the same one where the drug cookers had taken up residence during the time frame when the Lenoirs died. He would look into the exact location. "You never ran into anyone out there?"

She shook her head. "Never."

As they walked back into the living room, Branch studied the scene once more. The living room was located about midway between the front door and the back. If there was someone else in the house and they went out the back, as Sasha recalled, then they must have cut through the woods to get to where they had parked. Otherwise they would have had to go around front and to the main road and risk being seen by neighbors.

"How far through the woods until you reach another road?" he asked.

"Not that far. The woods are dense and there's probably a lot more undergrowth now since no one's been keeping it tramped down. For an adult running, maybe fifteen minutes. As a child it took a little longer."

Branch would follow up on where the shooters might have parked and, if they were lucky, someone who still lived nearby had seen someone. It wouldn't have mattered twenty-seven years ago because apparently no one was looking for a killer beyond the husband.

"Have you gone through the bedrooms?"

"I poked around a little. No serious digging."

Her arms went around herself as if she were cold and needed to protect herself from potential harm. She was tired and not entirely comfortable here, no matter that she wanted to appear strong and capable.

"Did coming here prompt any new memories?"

That was the real question. She hadn't been in this house since the night of the murders. It was possible seeing everything with new eyes had nudged one or more hidden memories.

"Nothing important that I didn't already know. There were two men in the house that night besides my father. I heard their voices. I'm almost certain there were two distinct voices." She shook her head. "My father didn't do this, Branch. No matter what the reports say and no matter how bizarre it sounds after all these years. My father did not kill anyone."

The thing was, he believed her.

Chapter Seven

Sasha chafed her arms to chase away the chill. Branch watched her so closely, his blue eyes seeming to see right through her. She wanted him to see her strength and determination but at the moment it felt as if all he saw was her fear that she wouldn't be able to prove what she believed in her heart.

And what if she was wrong?

No. She refused to believe her father had done this. Her entire life she had known, without doubt, that he was innocent. Now she had the opportunity to prove it and she was extremely fortunate to have Branch offering to help. Local law enforcement would lend far more credence to his investigation of an old case than to that of a member of the family—particularly the daughter determined to prove her father's innocence.

"Why don't we call it a day?" Branch glanced around. "You've taken in a lot today. Maybe let it filter tonight and start fresh tomorrow."

Not until that moment did Sasha realize how incredibly tired she was. It was as if his words somehow prompted her to relax, to stand down from the fight. "Good idea. I am unreasonably exhausted."

"I'll take you to dinner," he announced. "You can give me your thoughts on today's effort and I'll give you mine."

If she was smart she would pass. If she was smart she would go directly home, take a shower and hit the sack.

If she was smart she would recognize how very precarious this cliff upon which she had perched herself really was.

But she wasn't smart when it came to Branch Holloway and the past they shared.

"I'm not really dressed for going out." *Good job, Sash.* At least she tried, despite the idea that she felt herself leaning toward him, waiting for him to give her one good reason why her manner of dress didn't matter one little bit.

"The Back Porch is a great pub just off the town square." He looked her up and down, her skin heating with the move that even in an innocent moment like this one exuded sex appeal. "Nothing fancy, but great food."

There it was, the excuse she needed. "Well then, let me lock up here."

He followed her to the kitchen, where she locked the back door. "We can drop your rental off at your grandmother's and you can ride with me, if that's okay. No need to take both vehicles. Parking is sometimes at a premium."

She glanced at him. "Sure."

He trailed her back to the front door; she turned off the lights as she went. They stood on the porch while she locked the front door. No matter that it wasn't completely dark yet, it was utterly dark on the porch. The dense woods blocked the fading sunlight from reaching this far. She thought of all the times she had chased the looming shadows across the yard. She had never once been afraid here…not until that night.

When she was loaded in her car, he settled his hat into place and gave her a nod. "See you at your grandmother's."

Sasha gave him an answering nod. She told herself to smile but somehow being in the dark with Branch left her unable to do so. She rolled away from the gloomy house and the woods that held it hostage, and breathed a sigh of relief when she reached the main road. She felt as if she hadn't managed a deep breath since she set foot in that old house. All the dust, she told herself.

Layers and layers on top of the memories…the pieces of her life.

The drive to her grandmother's home was wrought with building tension. Hard as she tried not to, she had worked herself into an emotional frenzy by the time she parked in front of the house. She should have better control than this.

He hopped from his truck, skirted the hood and opened the passenger-side door for her.

Control? Ha! This was Branch Holloway. She'd never had any control when it came to him.

She climbed into the truck and he closed her door. All through her teenage years she had been besotted with him and he had barely acknowledged her existence beyond the Sunday lunches their grandmothers had shared. He slid behind the wheel of his truck, that big black cowboy hat of his lying on the seat between them. Of course, they'd run into each other outside school. Their grandmothers had been best friends. But he'd been two years older and always busy with football or being the most popular guy in school.

Sasha had been reasonably popular as a teenager. There were several difficult years right after her parents died but those may have been more about her inability to interact than about anyone else. She'd crept into a shell for a while. What child wouldn't under the circumstances?

A furtive glance in his direction had her gaze lingering there. He'd always had that perfect square jaw. The kind of face—particularly his lips—romance novel heroes were written about. Her daughter had those same lips as well as his blond hair and blue eyes. Brianne was the female version of Branch Holloway. So many times Sasha had wanted to tell her… had wanted to get out her old high school yearbooks and show off the child's handsome father.

But fear had kept her from doing so. Sasha, the woman who was fearless in every other aspect of her life, was terrified of what she had done and it was too late to fix that huge misstep.

Funny how she was here now, spending time with

Branch to try to rectify a part of her past, and she was keeping this life-altering part of his from him.

He would hate her when he learned that truth.

Her stomach roiled. Any appetite she had possessed vanished. What was she thinking? Allowing him to help her with this investigation would only make him feel used in the end. This had been a very bad idea.

Branch parked at the curb across the street from The Back Porch. Sasha recognized the corner shop. It had been an old antiques store the last time she was here. Now it was a happening place from all appearances. Lights were strung over the sidewalk on both street-facing sides of the establishment. Beyond the big windows tables were filled with patrons. Waitresses were running around with laden trays.

The passenger door opened before she realized Branch had gotten out of the truck and walked around to her side. He held out his hand and helped her down. She tugged at the hem of her tee and wished she had taken the time to change. He was right in that the place looked very casual, but she felt dusty and rumpled after plundering through her mother's office for so long.

"I can't say for sure what'll be on the menu tonight, but I can tell you that anything you order will be excellent."

She glanced at him, produced a smile. "Smells great." The aromas emanating from the screened entry doors had resurrected her appetite.

He smiled and her heart reacted. She looked

away. She spent her days and weeks managing other people's personal and professional crises and she couldn't keep her own ancient history under control? How sad was that?

Pull it together, Sash.

Branch opened the door and the music washed over them. A recent country hit, strumming through the sound system and through her. Inside, the floor was rustic, reclaimed wood as were the walls. A bar ran the length of the far wall. Every stool was occupied. Branch spoke to the waitress who looked up at him as if she was a mesmerized fan and he was her favorite rock star. Then she directed them to a table. It was tucked into a dark corner and Sasha was thankful for the out-of-the-way location.

The waitress took their drink orders; Branch suggested the house specialty—their craft beers. Sasha could use a beer to settle her nerves. Maybe she would sleep better, as well. Last night had been a battle with the covers all night. She'd awakened more tired than when she went to bed.

When the waitress returned with their beers, they ordered burgers and fries. Brianne would be appalled. She would strictly eat only healthy food. Sasha sipped her beer and relaxed. She loved that her daughter was so independent and strong-minded.

"How did your meeting go?" They had spent most of their time together talking about her and her parents; she felt bad that she had asked so few questions about him and his life.

He stared at the beer in his glass. "Great. It went

great. They made me a terrific offer for a position in Nashville—a promotion." He shrugged. "The whole thing went better than I expected."

Sasha laughed. "Wow. I have never heard a guy sound so down-and-out over such good news. Is this your excited face?"

He stared at her for a long moment, that mask of uncertainty not shifting the slightest. "I'm undecided. To tell you the truth, I like being close to my family. It's an unexpected development, that's for sure."

He sipped his beer and Sasha bit back the words she wanted to say. Branch was a good guy. He recognized that his parents and his grandmother were getting older and he felt compelled to stay close. This was just another perfect example of what made him so sweet. She, on the other hand, felt like scum. She hadn't once considered that it might be better if she moved closer to her grandmother. She was completely focused on her career and on her own life and that of her daughter.

"You should do what makes you happy, Branch." She turned the frosty beer glass round and round, kept her gaze focused on the rivulets of condensation sliding down the sides. "Too many people rush after the brass ring and lose out on happiness."

"Are you speaking from experience?"

Oh, damn. She'd said too much. She might as well confess now. "I have to say that I've considered the idea that I should have been here for my grandmother. I was the only family she had left and I was not around." If she'd hoped that confessing would make her feel better, she had been wrong.

Even after she'd found out she was pregnant, Sasha had been determined to forge her own life. She'd wanted to go far away from here and become someone else. Not the daughter of a man who had killed her mother and then himself.

"My grandmother always said your grandmother was very proud of you. She was very happy about your success. So don't go beating yourself up for something that wasn't real when she was alive and damned sure isn't real now. You're feeling guilty for a nonexistent issue."

She laughed. *God, if he only knew.* "So what are you, a shrink?"

He shook his head. "No. Just a guy with experience in the blame department."

No matter that she told herself she didn't want to know, she found herself asking, "What happened?"

"I broke protocol. Got involved with a witness and she died. My superiors cleared me of any blame in her death but that didn't seem to matter up here." He tapped his temple. "I still felt responsible. The two-week suspension for breaking protocol didn't seem like punishment enough."

"So you punish yourself by second-guessing whether or not you deserve this promotion."

The waitress arrived with their food before he could respond. Sasha poured a pool of ketchup on the edge of her plate and dragged a French fry through it. She nibbled the salty goodness. If she were completely honest she would admit that she devoted herself entirely to work and to her daughter because she didn't feel as if she deserved a personal life outside the relationship with her child. She lost that right when she gave up everyone who had been there for her during her life before college.

Her gaze drifted to the man across the table. Mostly because of him and how she'd left him out all these years.

They ate. Laughed at silly moments from high school. Shared the ways they had struggled to build their careers. When she'd devoured all she could hold of the best—bar none—hamburger she'd ever eaten and half a plate of fries, as well as a second beer, she asked the question that had been burning in the back of her mind for years.

"Why no wife or kids? And don't give me that ridiculous answer you gave before about letting the only one for you get away."

He shrugged. "Hey, it's true." He sipped his ice water. No second beer for him since he was driving. "How was I supposed to fall in love with someone else when you stole my heart when I was fifteen."

She rolled her eyes. "That is completely not true and certainly no answer."

He pushed his plate away. "I guess I just never ran upon anyone who made me want that kind of relationship. What about you? What went wrong with your daughter's father? The two of you aren't still together. Maybe you let the only one for you get away, too."

Fear pounded in her veins. "We were never together." She stared at her plate, tried to think what to say next. "I...I screwed that one up. He was a good guy but he's...he's out of the picture." She met his gaze then. "I made a mess of everything and my daughter is paying the price."

A frown of concern lined his handsome face. "There's nothing you can do to work things out? He doesn't sound like such a good guy to me if he's not interested in having a relationship with his daughter."

Sasha felt as if she couldn't breathe. She had to change the subject. Now. "I visited the guy who fired my dad. Polk, Dennis Polk."

Branch angled his head, studied her face for a long moment. Then picked up on her cue, her change of subject. "What did he have to say?"

"He didn't fire my dad permanently." She explained how Polk had tried to handle the situation. Her tension eased a little as they drifted back onto safer ground. "The interesting thing was, he doesn't believe my father killed my mother either."

She also told him about her conversation with the Martins. A brief pause was required while the waitress cleared their table and asked about dessert, which they both declined. Branch insisted on paying. Another point of contention. She could not have him paying for her meals as if they were on a date. *This was not a date.*

"You were busy today." He leaned forward, braced his forearms on the table. "I'd like you to keep me informed of where you are and what you're doing from now on. Just to be safe."

She stared at him for a long moment, hoping to ascertain the motive for the statement. "Are you or Chief Brannigan concerned with my activities?"

Branch held up his hands. "No way. I just want to know you're okay." His arms dropped back to the table. "We have to face the fact that if your father didn't do this, someone else did. Whoever that someone else is, chances are they don't want us learning their secret."

It was a valid point. Certainly the idea had crossed her mind but she had chosen not to be put off by it. "What if that person or persons is dead?"

"Then we probably have nothing to worry about but we're talking about cold-blooded murder. A well-thought-out-and-executed set of murders. This was no impulse kill or robbery. It was planned carefully and carried out mercilessly. That tells us a number of things. First, someone powerful may have been involved—as in someone who paid hired professional thugs to do the dirty work. Or someone close to your family who knew the details of their daily lives and who could get in and out without being caught."

Planned and executed. She reminded herself to breathe. He was right. The images conjured by his words made her stomach clench and the taste of the burger she'd eaten turned bitter. Their deaths had not been about a robbery. Nothing had been missing—at least nothing of which anyone was aware. Certainly not money or jewelry or the usual valuables.

"Let's exchange contact information."

Once their cell numbers were added to each other's contact list, she asked, "So what do we do now?"

"We create a list of potential suspects. Anyone who was involved in the lives of your parents, either professionally or personally. Someone who had something to lose if a particular event occurred." His broad shoulders lifted and fell in a slight shrug. "We can probably rule out Polk. If he was in love with your mother, it's unlikely he would have killed her. The more reasonable path would have been to try to get your father out of the way."

"We might as well list everyone living in Winchester at the time." She rubbed at her forehead. The idea was overwhelming. "This is a small town, Branch. Everyone knows everyone else."

He nodded. "True. But not everyone has something to gain at the expense of someone else. This is what we need to find. What did your parents know or have that was worth killing for?"

She shook her head. "I should have made my grandmother talk about this. She refused when I was growing up. She said it was too painful. But I should have pushed the issue in recent years. Now she's gone."

Sasha rested her face in her hands. This was too much. Too, too much.

"Hey." Long fingers wrapped around one of her hands and tugged it away from her face. Blue eyes zoomed in on hers. "We'll figure this out. One step at a time. If you look at the big picture it can be overwhelming."

She dropped her free hand to her lap and told herself to pull her hand away from his but her body refused to obey. The sensation of his long fingers encircling hers made her feel safe and warm and not so lost and alone in this misery.

"We're going to look at this one piece at a time. We'll start with their personal lives. We dissect each piece. Were there financial issues? Had your grandmother been helping financially? I'll talk to my grandmother and see what she knows—if anything—that might help."

"Why are we starting with their personal lives first?" As a crisis manager, Sasha knew the value of a marketable commodity. For most people that was their professional lives. Certainly with celebrities the two often intertwined but the concept was the same. No matter that her grandmother liked to laughingly disagree, money—or the lack thereof—was usually the root of real trouble.

"This was up close and personal. Not a drive-by or a long-distance kill. Up close. Personal. There was intense passion behind these murders."

Sasha stared at him for a long moment; her hand felt cold despite the feel of his skin against hers. "Is that why the police were so convinced the killer was my father?"

Branch nodded. "In situations like this, it's almost always the husband."

"But not this time."

"I firmly do not believe your father killed your mother," he agreed.

There was a *but* coming. She could see it in his face, hear it in his voice.

"*But* there's a strong possibility the reason they both ended up dead is because of something your father knew or had done. This would be why he pleaded so for her life. He didn't want her to die for something he had done."

She drew her hand away from his, his skin suddenly burning hers. "I see your point, but I'll reserve judgment until we have more facts."

Sasha had spent her entire life believing her father was innocent. She wasn't about to throw him under the bus from a different perspective at this point without substantial evidence.

"Reserving judgment is warranted," he acquiesced. "We should both keep an open mind until we have all the facts—or as many as we can dig up."

"All right." She clasped her hands together in her lap. "Are you certain you have the time to devote to this case? I know you're on vacation and obviously you have a decision to make."

Sasha stopped herself. What was she doing? Could she really spend the next several days working so closely with Branch without resurrecting those old feelings? Of course not. She was already struggling. Instead, she should be trying to figure out how she was going to tell him about Brianne. She had waited a very long time to find the truth. She didn't want to screw it up now.

What a mess she had made.

He started to answer her question but she held up her hands to stop him. "I'm sorry. I shouldn't be asking you to do this. You've been far too kind and giving already. This isn't your issue. It's mine. You have a life and I shouldn't be dragging you into my problems."

He chuckled but there was no humor in the sound, more a sad weariness. "First, I offered to help because I would very much like to be a part of resolving this case. Second, I have nothing else I need to do except make that career decision in the next few days about where I go from here. Seriously, I am totally available."

"Still," she argued, "this is too complicated, too personal..."

"I want to do this, Sasha. It means a lot to me. Your family means a lot to me."

She wished he hadn't said those words. Tears brimmed on her lashes before she could stop them. "I don't have any extended family left, Branch."

He grinned. "You have your daughter and you have me and my family."

"You're right. I'm feeling sorry for myself and I should get over it and get the job done."

He winked. "That's what I want to hear."

He stood. "Come on. I'll take you home. We have a lot to do tomorrow."

The drive to her grandmother's house was quiet

but it was a comfortable silence. Sasha felt content with the decisions they had made. When he'd parked in front of the house and reached for his door, she stopped him with a hand on his arm.

"Now *I* have some ground rules."

He nodded. "All right."

"I don't need you to walk me to the door and I can open my own door." When he would have argued, she held up a hand and went on. "It's not that I don't appreciate it, but it's not necessary. Also, I pay for my own meals."

He made a face. "You're being unreason—"

"No exceptions. Tomorrow I pay since you paid tonight."

He held up his hands in surrender. "Fine."

"I don't mind keeping you informed of where I am—it makes sense. But I am a strong woman, Branch. I am completely capable of taking care of myself."

He nodded. "Got it."

"Thank you." She reached for her door. "Good night. I'll see you in the morning."

"Good night."

She climbed out of his truck, closed the door and walked straight to the front door without looking back. He didn't leave until she had unlocked the door and gone inside. She supposed she couldn't complain about that part.

Inside, she leaned against the door and closed her eyes to slow the spinning in her head. She really was in trouble here. She wanted Branch Holloway in a completely selfish way.

Sasha had developed a reputation for never giving in or giving up. She was relentless. Other than her time with her daughter, she had no personal life. Honestly, she could not remember the last time she'd been intimate. She wasn't an idiot. She understood the core issue at play here. Years of depriving herself had made her weak, had caused her to be vulnerable.

This was not a good time to be vulnerable.

But Branch made her want things she shouldn't want. All he had to do was walk into the room. He didn't even have to look at her. The very act of breathing was somehow sexy on him.

"Idiot."

Sasha pushed away from the door, locked it and headed upstairs. She needed to hear Brianne's voice, and then she intended to have a long hot bath and to get some sleep.

Whatever else tomorrow brought, she had to be prepared for spending time with the man without making a mistake that would impact her daughter.

She'd already made one too many of those.

Chapter Eight

Sasha's eyes opened.

It was still dark. She reached for her cell on the bedside table.

2:06 glowed from the screen.

She closed her eyes and told her brain to go back to sleep. It was too early.

The whisper of a sound, the slide of a rubber sole across a wood floor, fabric swiped against a painted wall. Just a little swoosh.

Her eyes flew open again.

This time the darkness closed in on her, squashing the air from her lungs.

Heart pounding, she sat up, grabbed her cell. Her fingers instantly poised to enter 911.

Wait. She needed to take a breath and listen. Ensure she hadn't dreamed the sounds. She struggled to calm her racing heart and to quiet the sound of blood roaring through her veins.

The squeak of a floorboard…another soft whisper of a footfall.

Someone was definitely in the house.

She tapped Branch's name in her contact list as she hurried soundlessly across the room. Holding her breath, she opened the closet door. Thank God it didn't squeak. She burrowed as deeply inside as possible, pulling the door soundlessly shut behind her.

"Hey—" Branch's voice echoed sleepily in her ear "—what's up?"

She turned her back to the door and whispered, "Someone is in the house."

"Hang up and call 911. I'll be right there."

She did as he asked and tried to flatten herself against the back wall behind the clothes from high school that still hung in her closet.

The dispatcher came on the line with her practiced spiel. Sasha gave her address and situation.

"Officers are on the way to your home, Ms. Lenoir. Where in the house are you?"

"Second floor, third door on the left. I'm in the closet."

"Good. Are you armed?"

Another brush of sound. This one on the stairs.

"What?" she murmured.

The dispatcher repeated the question.

"No." What she would give for a weapon. "Wait." Sasha used her free hand to feel through the darkness until her fingers tightened on the item she hoped to find. "I have my baton."

It was the baton she'd used in junior high. Just

over two feet long and with a classic star ball on each end. A whack to the face or chest or private area could disable a man.

As long as he didn't have a gun.

Her fingers tightened around the baton.

Pounding echoed through the house.

Sasha's heart nearly stalled.

"Sasha! It's Branch. I'm coming in."

The door was locked. How would he get in?

"The police are turning into your driveway now, Ms. Lenoir."

Sasha tried to think. "US Marshal Branch Holloway is at the front door. I called him first. Should I go down and let him in?"

"Stay where you are, ma'am."

"Sasha!"

She couldn't just stay hidden like this. She opened the door and eased out of the closet. The moonlight coming in through the window had her blinking after being in total darkness for several minutes.

Standing very still, she listened for sound. Besides Branch's pounding she heard nothing else.

She burst out of her room and rushed down the stairs. "I'm coming."

A crash in the kitchen froze her feet to the floor.

For a single second she wanted to run after the sound. Good sense took over and she rushed to the front door instead and unlocked it for Branch.

"Are you all right?"

"Yes. I heard something in the kitchen just now."

"Stay close behind me."

Sasha fell into step right behind him. He flipped lights on as they went. Once in the kitchen he stopped. She bumped into his back.

"The back door is standing open," Branch said.

Sasha leaned past his shoulder, saw a uniformed police officer coming through the wide-open door. She had locked that door. She was certain of it.

"My partner's going over the yard," the officer said. "Are you clear in here?"

"I'll make sure. You take the exterior."

The officer disappeared into the darkness. That was when Sasha saw Branch's weapon.

Her breath caught.

Branch reached back with his free hand and gave her arm a squeeze. "I want you to stay close behind me while we look around inside. I'm confident the intruder is gone but let's not take any chances."

It wasn't until they had cleared the dining room and family room as well as the powder room that she realized she had dropped her cell phone. It lay on the floor at the bottom of the stairs.

She grabbed it. "I don't think he came upstairs. I think that was his intention but your pounding on the front door stopped him."

As they climbed, Branch asked, "Do you have reason to believe the intruder was a he?"

"Well, no. I'm just assuming."

"He didn't speak or make any sounds?"

"I heard the sound of his clothing brushing the wall or a piece of furniture and the whisper of his shoe soles on the floor."

"What woke you up?" He entered the first bedroom, the one her grandmother had always used for a guest room.

"I guess the sound of him moving about downstairs. I thought I imagined it, so I tried to go back to sleep. Then I heard it again. Really soft sounds."

They checked each room and found nothing.

"Now let's have a look downstairs and see if anything is missing?"

"Okay."

One side of his mouth hitched up into a grin. "Nice weapon."

Her fingers loosened slightly on the baton. "One of the girls on my team knocked a guy out with her baton."

He laughed. "I think I remember hearing about that. Gave him a concussion, didn't she?"

"That part was a rumor, I think."

"Marshal Holloway, I'm coming in."

Sasha turned toward the front door as it opened and one of the officers stepped inside. Since Branch was armed, the officer announcing his intentions was a smart move.

"We have a secondary scene outside."

Sasha wasn't certain what the term *secondary scene* meant but she was confident it wasn't a good thing.

"Stay inside with Ms. Lenoir and I'll have a look."

"Excuse me," she protested. "I would like to see this secondary scene, as well."

Branch looked to the officer, who said, "The yard is clear, Marshal."

"Take a second look around inside," Branch suggested. "Ms. Lenoir and I will talk to your partner outside."

"Yes, sir."

"Stay close," Branch cautioned again.

She followed him outside, down the steps and around the corner of the house. Obviously this secondary scene was in the backyard. The other uniformed officer was waiting near the porch.

"The perpetrator entered through the rear door," the young man, who couldn't be more than twenty-five, said. "There's evidence the lock was disabled."

"Good work, Officer Gabrielle. What else did you find?"

Gabrielle shone his flashlight onto the wall near the far end of the porch. Words had been spray-painted on the siding.

You were supposed to die that night...

For several seconds Sasha could only stare at the words; they wouldn't assimilate in her brain... Then suddenly they did. Her heart bumped against her sternum.

"I think you can safely say that you've kicked a hornet's nest," Branch announced.

Where's the kid? the man with the deep voice demanded.

At a friend's. She's not here. Her mother's voice. Terror pulsed in every syllable. *She's a child. She doesn't know anything!*

Sasha turned to Branch. "Whoever left that message was in the house that night. He knows I was supposed to die, too, but my mother told them I was at a friend's."

A sinking feeling had her knees going weak. Sasha steadied herself. At least now there was no question about what happened that night and it was no longer only dependent upon her unreliable memories. This was evidence.

Someone had murdered her parents.

DAYLIGHT HAD ARRIVED by the time the evidence collectors had come and gone. Sasha had made two pots of coffee and dragged out the leftover pastries from the gathering on Sunday evening.

She stood in the backyard staring at the words that had been sprayed with red spray paint. *You were supposed to die that night...*

Why did it matter to her parents' killer if she lived or died?

What could she have possibly known that counted for anything?

Had she seen the killer before? Was it someone she knew when she was a child?

She needed more coffee. In the dining room the pastries were mostly gone but there was still coffee. She'd had to set up in the dining room since the kitchen was a crime scene.

Crime scene.

She shuddered. No one should have to go through something like that twice in a lifetime. In New York she had a security system. Maybe she should have one installed here.

Should she sell the house at the same time she sold the Lenoir home place?

She hadn't really thought that far into the future. She had to talk to Brianne. This was her legacy, too.

Sasha poured the coffee and went back outside via the front door. Halfway around the house she ran into Branch and another man wearing a cowboy hat. Wait—she knew him. She just couldn't place his face.

"Sasha, this is Chief of Police Billy Brannigan."

She extended her hand. "I remember you. You played football for Tennessee."

"I did." He gave her hand a quick shake.

All of Winchester had celebrated when he made the cut. "Did your forensic people find anything useful?"

"Well—" he pushed his hat up a little and settled his hands on his hips "—it's too early to tell just yet, but I did want to speak with you about the case you and Branch are investigating."

Sasha glanced at Branch.

"We should talk inside," he offered.

Sasha led the way to the family room. She closed the French doors to the dining room as well as the door to the kitchen. She turned back to the two men waiting for her attention.

"Why don't we sit," Brannigan offered.

"Of course." Sasha hadn't had nearly enough sleep. Her brain was hardly working.

They settled around the coffee table, Branch on

the sofa with her, Brannigan in the chair directly across from them.

"Ms. Lenoir—"

"Sasha," she protested.

"Sasha," he amended, "it's clear you've awakened a sleeping bear."

That was one way to put it. "It's also clear that my father didn't kill my mother or himself."

"I certainly believe we have justifiable cause to officially reopen the case."

Sasha barely restrained a cheer.

"We've established more than justifiable cause, Chief," Branch argued. "We've proven reasonable doubt in the initial findings. If there were any questions, the message outside should have alleviated those."

Brannigan nodded. "I agree, but I also understand that there are plenty of folks who like to stir trouble. It's possible someone you've spoken to—" this he said to Sasha "—has decided to give legs to your case. Folks were divided twenty-seven years ago. There were those who believed your daddy was guilty and those who were certain he was innocent. Your digging around in the past is the perfect opportunity to turn the tide of things in the direction they believed was the right one to begin with."

As much as Sasha wanted to dispute his assertion, his conclusion was reasonable and logical. Even in a small town people took sides in controversies, especially those that involved lifelong members of the community and murder.

"What're you suggesting we do moving forward?" Branch asked, his tone as pointed as his expression. He obviously wasn't happy with where this was going.

Sasha spoke first. "Chief, I respect your thoughts on the matter but I have every intention of continuing my search for the truth. I'm well aware that as long as I don't break any laws or cause any obstruction of any sort that I can do as I please."

Branch turned his hands up. "I'm on vacation and I intend to help her do exactly that—in a completely unofficial capacity, of course."

Brannigan looked from one to the other. "Well, I won't waste my time trying to talk you out of it. I will, however, need the case file back so I can re-open the investigation."

"Do we have time to make a copy?"

Brannigan's lips formed a grim line. "It was one thing when this was a cold case, Branch. This is now an official police investigation. I can't have copies all over the place. We should step back and do this right. You know the drill as well as I do. Whatever we find, we don't want a simple technicality to cause trouble in the courtroom."

"I understand," Branch conceded. "The case file is at my house. I'll have it at your office before noon."

Sasha wanted to argue with him but decided to save her frustration for when it was just the two of them. A united front was what she needed right now. She was an outsider, no matter how many years her family had resided here. Branch was one of them and he was a member of law enforcement. Besides, the case file wasn't at his house; it was here. She trusted that he had good reason for not sharing that information with the chief.

In the end, they would figure this out, with or without the file.

"Thanks, Branch. I'll make sure Cindy is on the lookout for it. I'll have a meeting with my detectives and get the ball rolling and I'll keep you informed as well as I can."

"I appreciate it, Billy."

Brannigan stood and settled his hat back into place. "Thank you for your cooperation, Ms. Lenoir." He nodded to her and then to the other man. "Branch."

Branch followed him to the front door. Sasha strained to hear anything one or both might say.

"Keep an eye on her, Branch," Brannigan warned. "Obviously there is some danger here. I'm not sure she understands how complicated this could get."

"I'll keep her safe," Branch guaranteed. "A situation like this morning won't happen again."

When Branch returned to the family room, Sasha opened her mouth to protest having to turn over the file without a copy but Branch held up his hand for her to wait. He went back to the entry hall and checked out the window. When he returned to where she waited, he kept his voice low.

"We have a few minutes before Billy will become suspicious. Where's the case file?"

"In my bedroom. I put it in the closet." She shrugged. "Just in case."

"Good idea."

As they climbed the stairs, she whispered to him, "If he won't allow us to make a copy—"

"We can't make a copy but he didn't say anything about taking photos."

Sasha smiled for the first time today. "Smart thinking."

At the top of the stairs he paused, held her gaze. "I've been doing this a while. Never count me out."

She would know never to do that again. "Thanks."

During the next few minutes they snapped pics with their cells. Every page, every photo. Sasha's stomach churned as she took care of the crime scene photos. When the last one was complete, Branch repacked the files into the box.

"I'll tuck this back in your closet and pick it up on my way to Billy's office later today."

She nodded her understanding. Before she could ask what was next, he said, "Pack a bag. You're not staying here alone anymore."

"Where are you suggesting I stay?"

"You're staying with me." He carried the file box to her closet, deposited it on the floor and covered it with the same throw she'd had over it.

For a moment she only stared at him. He couldn't possibly think she would stay with him at his house... *alone*.

"I know what you're thinking." He tapped her on the temple. "Don't fight me on this, Sasha. Besides my grandmother, I'm the only one who's completely on your side in this."

"I can stay at a motel or at the inn." She wasn't actually sure of what establishments still operated in Winchester. Good grief. She could not spend time under the same roof with him. Not the way he was suggesting.

"Look. This is not some plot to take advantage of you. You can stay at my grandmother's if you prefer. I just don't want you alone at night—anywhere. We can use the evenings to go over what we find and compare notes and thoughts. We'll spend most evenings together anyway."

So maybe he had a point. "You have a guest room?"

"I do. You can take my room since it's upstairs. I'll take the guest room downstairs. There will be an entire floor between us."

Now she just felt foolish. "Well, all right. I'll pack a few things."

"Good." He nodded. "I'll get out of your way."

Somewhere downstairs the sound of her cell phone ringing pierced the air.

Sasha headed for the door. "That's my phone."

"You pack. I'll get your phone."

She nodded. "Thanks."

With her smallest suitcase opened on the bed, she started layering in sleepwear and clothes. She groaned when she realized she'd been running around all morning in a nightshirt. At least she'd had the good sense to pull on one of her grandmother's sweaters once Branch had arrived.

"What a night," she grumbled.

"Mom?"

The sound of her daughter's voice reverberated up the stairs. Sasha's heart nearly stopped.

"I'm not your mom, but I'm taking the phone to her. Hold on a minute."

"Who are you?"

Sasha winced. That was her daughter's interested tone. She probably thought— Sasha shook her head. She didn't want to go there.

"I'm US Marshal Branch Holloway, an old friend of your mom's."

He walked into the room, grinning from ear to ear.

Sasha reached out; her hand trembled in spite of her struggle to keep it steady. "Thanks."

He placed the phone in her hand, her daughter's pic filling the screen. Her blond hair and blue eyes exact duplicates of his.

"I'll be waiting downstairs."

Sasha nodded. Not trusting her voice. When he'd left the room she took the phone off Speaker and said, "Hey, baby."

"Who was that?"

Sasha collapsed onto the bed. "An old friend, sweetie. He's helping with all this stuff that needs to be done." She had not told her daughter about her search into the past. Until she had some evidence one way or another, there was no point sharing any of this with anyone beyond official personnel. Though, technically, she did have some evidence now.

"Mom, he sounds hot. You should live a little. I'm doing a Google search on him right now."

Sasha's mouth went dry. "You know how photos on the internet are never like the real person."

"So when are you coming home?"

Sasha managed her first deep breath since her phone rang. "Next week, I hope."

"I don't understand why I can't come there. There was a death in the family. I can make up the homework and tests."

"We'll talk about that later in the week."

"OMG, he is straight fire."

"Why aren't you on your way to school?" Her heart was hammering again.

"Okay, okay. Chill. I won't be late."

In the background Sasha heard Avery's voice urging Brianne to hurry before she was late. Saved by the nanny!

Thank God.

"I'll talk to you after school, sweetie."

"Okay. Love you!"

"Love you, too."

The call ended but Sasha's heart didn't stop pounding. Her daughter had seen a photo of her father.

Branch had seen a photo of his daughter.

Sasha was running out of time and someone had threatened her life.

She stood. She couldn't control precisely how the investigation of this case went, but she could still navigate the other. She would not leave her daughter in the dark the way her grandmother had left her.

All she had to do was find the right moment to tell her the truth. First, she needed to tell Branch.

Chapter Nine

Arlene Holloway had come to her grandson's house as soon as she heard the news. She also insisted on throwing together a late breakfast. Sasha tried to help but the eighty-five-year-old woman shooed her away. So while Arlene prepared eggs and toast and bacon, Sasha and Branch discussed where to go next with their investigation.

"Come and get it!"

By the time they wandered into Branch's kitchen, Arlene had already arranged her own plate and was stationed at the head of the kitchen table.

Sasha had been certain she couldn't eat. Not after all that had happened this morning. Apparently her emotional reaction had been a little delayed. By the time they had driven from her house to Branch's, she was trembling and feeling weak-kneed. She hated feeling frail, hated even more for anyone to witness the episode.

"That's the way it always worked for me," the older woman had said. "I was always the one who could keep it together during a crisis, but then when it was over I fell apart."

Weathering crises was Sasha's brand. No one was better, but she had definitely had trouble holding herself together after they left her grandmother's home. Sasha understood the reason this situation was different was because it was personal. At work she was dealing with other people's crises. This was profoundly private and it went all the way back to her childhood.

"I've been thinking about what you asked me," Arlene announced, her attention moving from her freshly emptied plate to the man at the other end of the table.

"Did you think of anyone?" Branch asked.

Sasha looked from him to his grandmother.

"Your mother," she said to Sasha, "had lots of friends. She was a very busy lady, all about work, so she didn't do a lot of socializing. But there was one friend she lunched with fairly regularly. Vi and I some-times ran into them at the diner."

"Is her name Penny or Patty?" For the life of her, Sasha could not recall the name. She was glad Branch had remembered to ask his grandmother.

"Not a Penny or a Patty. That's why I had to do some thinking. The name was wrong. It's Leandra Brennan. Her friends called her Lenny."

"Lenny." The name clicked. Sasha nodded. "That's it. Is this woman still alive?"

"She is. Still lives in the same house and works at the same job. Her house is over on North High

Street. Six-oh-six. You probably won't find her at home on a workday though. She's Jarvis Packard's personal assistant."

"Jarvis Packard?" The name wasn't familiar to Sasha. She'd been gone a very long time.

"The biggest land developer in the Southeast," Branch said. He pushed his cleaned plate away. "His company is involved in any major project that happens in the area."

"Where're the Packard offices?"

"Over on South College," Arlene said. "You can't miss it. There's a huge sign."

Arlene scooted back her chair and stood. "Now you two get on about your business and I'll clean up here."

"Gran," Branch argued, "you've already done too much."

"Your mama told me to take care of you while she and your daddy are on vacation."

"I don't think she intended for you to cook for me," he protested as he took his plate to the sink.

Sasha followed with her own plate and fork. She loved hearing the two bicker. It was so cute to see the big fearless marshal concede to his little old grandmother. Sasha rinsed the dishes and tucked them into the dishwasher. Arlene wiped the table.

"You planning to visit Lenny?" Arlene asked.

"I am," Sasha confirmed. "If she was my mother's closest friend, perhaps she'll know if there was something unusual happening around the time of the murders."

It felt suddenly odd to speak about the murders in such an investigative manner. Twenty-seven years had elapsed since that night. Sasha had long ago come to terms with the pain of shock and loss. The events of that night had left lifelong wounds with deep scars. But she had chosen to move forward despite the trauma.

Now those emotions resurfaced with the same raw ache she'd felt as a child.

"I can go with you," Branch offered.

Arlene sent him a frown. "I doubt she will want to talk in front of you. Heavens, Branch, you know better than that. If the woman knows anything, she's far more likely to tell her friend's daughter than some lawman."

"She has a point," Sasha agreed.

"I'll follow you there on my way to see Luther Holcomb."

"Luther?" Arlene pushed the last chair into the table. "He was convinced your daddy did the killing, Sasha. He refused to see that night any other way. I remember arguing with him but it did no good whatsoever."

This was the part that nagged at Sasha. All her adult life she had ignored this aspect of the past but now it was simply impossible to ignore. "Why didn't my grandmother argue with him? Why didn't she fight for the truth?"

Arlene seemed to shrink into herself—as if the question had shaken her. Sasha immediately felt contrite for her poor choice in words.

"I think she wanted to protect you? The longer the investigation dragged out, the harder it was for you to move on. Like she said, *dead is dead*. No amount of hollering and screaming and making a fuss was going to bring her daughter back."

Sasha considered for the first time how painful her mother's death must have been for her grandmother. Alexandra had been Sasha's mother, but she had been Viola's only child. Sasha couldn't fathom even the concept of losing her own daughter.

"I can understand how she wanted to put the hurt behind her—behind the both of us." She pushed the painful thought away and turned to Branch. "I guess we should get started."

He nodded. "I need to talk to Luther," he explained, "before the official investigation shuts him down to those not part of that investigation."

"We'll connect after our meetings," Sasha said. She could do this part on her own. Besides, they could get a lot more done going their separate ways.

He pointed a finger at her. "I want to know where you are at all times. When you leave one location headed to another, I want to know."

"I expect the same," she tossed back at him.

He grabbed his hat and settled it into place. "You got it."

"Thanks for breakfast, Mrs. Holloway." Sasha gave the lady a hug.

She patted Sasha on the back. "Your mama would be very proud of you."

The words haunted Sasha all the way across town.

Her grandmother had told her often enough as a child that her mother would be proud of her, but Sasha hadn't considered how her mother would feel about her reopening this investigation.

"The truth is what matters," Sasha said aloud as she turned into the parking lot of the Packard building.

She watched Branch continue on South College. Sasha wasn't sure where former chief of police Luther Holcomb lived now. Her attention settled on the six-story building with the huge *P* on top that had not been here when she was a kid.

Sasha climbed out of the rental, tucked the strap of her bag on her shoulder and headed for the main entrance. She couldn't be sure if this Lenny person was at work today, if she was out of town on vacation or tied up in back-to-back meetings, but Sasha had to try.

Inside, the elegant lobby was massive with towering ceilings and a wall of plants behind the elegant reception desk. The other three walls were tinted glass. Sleek tile floors, combined with all the glass, gave the lobby a cold feel. The neatly arranged pit of leather seating didn't help.

Cold and austere.

Sasha was glad she'd chosen a gray sweater to wear with her jeans today. She didn't exactly look professional but she did look casually comfortable. She'd tucked her long, curly hair into a clip.

When the receptionist ended her call and looked up, Sasha smiled. "I'm here to see Leandra Brennan."

A practiced smile that didn't quite reach her eyes slid into place. "Do you have an appointment?"

"No," Sasha confessed. "I'm only in town for a few days and I thought I'd drop in. I'm Alexandra Lenoir's daughter. If you would just tell her I'm here."

"I can call her office and see if she's available," the receptionist offered.

"Thank you."

Rather than sit, Sasha wandered to the far side of the lobby where a freestanding glass wall featured ongoing and upcoming projects. A new mall in Tullahoma. A hotel near the interstate. A medical complex by the Winchester hospital. Packard was apparently involved in anything big in the tri-county area.

"Ms. Lenoir—" the receptionist's carefully modulated tone reached out "—Mrs. Brennan can see you now."

Surprised but thankful, Sasha went through the steps. She provided her driver's license and stood still for a photo. Then she was given the code for the ride upstairs. On the elevator she entered the code and the doors automatically closed and the car bumped into motion, stopping on the top floor.

As cold and austere as the lobby was, the top floor was anything but. Thick carpeting, rich wall colors and lavish furnishings. Another receptionist looked up from her desk and smiled.

"Please have a seat. Mrs. Brennan will be with you shortly."

"Thank you."

Sasha settled into a plush upholstered chair and worked on relaxing. She wanted to appear calm and intelligent, not emotional and desperate. This could be the step that made all the difference in discovering the truth she so badly wanted to find. If she had harbored any reservations about this endeavor, she certainly did not after last night's intruder. Someone knew what she was doing and that someone was worried. That had to mean something.

You were supposed to die that night...

Had her grandmother feared for her own and Sasha's lives? Was that why she hadn't pursued a different conclusion from the official one reached by the police department? Her grandmother had been a very intelligent woman. She would have realized that nothing added up. The concept that Viola Simmons might have been afraid shook Sasha. Her grandmother had always appeared so brave and strong.

But everyone had his or her breaking point. Sasha could not imagine surviving the loss of a child. Arlene was right. Viola's entire focus would have been on protecting Sasha.

Whatever it took, she would find the truth—for her parents and for her grandmother. Sasha's grandfather on her mother's side had died before Sasha was born, so she had never known him. She had heard stories that he was a shrewd businessman, which was why her grandmother had never had to worry financially. Her father's parents and sister had moved away after the murders. Sasha had never once heard from them. She supposed they had been too devastated. But she had been a child and they shouldn't have abandoned her.

She had considered contacting them but she'd never pursued any search. If they hadn't cared about what happened to her, then she'd just as soon leave well enough alone. Unless they had information about what had happened?

Why would they not have stayed and fought for justice if they believed her father was innocent? Or had some proof?

Why hadn't someone done the right thing?

"Sasha."

Sasha looked up at the sound of the woman's voice. The red hair and blue eyes instantly triggered memories of her mother and this woman—a younger version of this woman—huddled over magazines and talking about decorating.

She stood and extended her hand. "Thank you for taking the time to see me, Ms. Brennan."

The woman nodded. "Let's go to my office."

Sasha followed her down the hall and into an office with a massive window; though the view of South College and the parking lot wasn't that spectacular, it did allow lots of light. The furnishings were elegant and numerous accolades lined the walls.

Brennan loosened a button on her suit jacket and settled into the chair behind her desk. She wore her hair down over her shoulders as she had decades ago. The gray streaks reminded Sasha just how much time had passed.

"Please—" the older woman gestured to the chairs opposite her desk "—have a seat."

Sasha perched on the edge of a wingback. Suddenly she felt nervous. Perhaps it was foolish but she felt as if what this woman had to say could be a turning point in her search for the truth.

"You look well," Brennan said. "I was sorry to hear about your grandmother. She was a kind and gracious woman."

"Thank you. It was a blow." There was no other way to put it. Losing her grandmother had shaken Sasha's world. Perhaps that was why she was here as much as for any other reason.

"I hear you've made quite the name for yourself in New York." Brennan smiled. "Your mother would be proud."

Sasha nodded, the burn of emotion suddenly attacking her eyes. She really needed to get a hold on herself. "I'm good at what I do."

"And you have a daughter. I understand she's quite the dancer. I'm sure you have your sights set on Juilliard."

Sasha wanted to ask if Brennan had remained close with her grandmother but it didn't feel right. Why wouldn't her grandmother have mentioned talking to Brennan?

"She does," Sasha allowed. "Personally I have my hopes set on Columbia or Princeton."

Brennan nodded. "Sometimes things don't turn out the way we expect."

There was a sadness in her eyes and her voice as she said the words.

"No one knows that better than me," Sasha agreed. "One day my life was the perfect nine-year-old's world and the next my parents were dead. Murdered."

Brennan blinked. "It was a tragedy."

"My mother was worried about something those last few days of her life," Sasha lied. She actually had no recall of her mother being upset about anything except her father's job issue. "You were helping her. I remember you calling and leaving her a message."

Fear or something on that order flashed in the other woman's eyes before she schooled the reaction. "Perhaps you didn't know that your parents were having a difficult time. Your father had lost his job and they were arguing a lot. I tried to be there for her but I'm afraid I failed her miserably. If I'd had any idea Brandon would go that far I would have done something. The fact is, I was out of town on business for days before and after…that night."

"Is that why the police didn't interview you?" It seemed strange to Sasha that the police would not have interviewed the victim's best friend.

"I suppose so. Why do you ask?"

One aspect of Sasha's work that she was particularly good at was reading her clients. It was extremely important that she recognize when one was lying. It wasn't that she took only clients who were honest and aboveboard—that wasn't the case at all. But she didn't take clients who lied to *her*.

Leandra Brennan was lying.

"Oh." Sasha frowned. "I guess you haven't heard."

Brennan frowned as if she had no idea what Sasha meant.

"Chief Brannigan is reopening the case. New evidence has come to light that suggests my father was innocent. In fact, the same person who murdered my mother murdered him, as well."

Blink. Blink. Shock. "What new evidence?"

Sasha sighed. "I'm afraid I'm not at liberty to discuss it. I can tell you that someone broke into my grandmother's house last night and left me a threatening message. It wasn't pleasant. The chief feels that's all the more indication that the new investigation is on the right track."

Sasha hoped the other woman wasn't so good at ferreting out untruths because she had just woven an elaborate tale that was only partly true.

Brennan put her hand to her chest. "That's terrible—about the break-in, I mean. I'm glad you're all right. What kind of message did the intruder leave?"

Sasha held her gaze for a long moment, mostly to drag out the tension. "He said I should have died that night. I guess the killers didn't realize I was hiding under the stairs and heard everything." She shook her head. "There were two of them in the house. It's a shame Chief Holcomb didn't listen to me all those years ago or my parents' killers wouldn't have gotten away with murder."

"I had no idea." Brennan's words were cold and stilted.

"No one did. But now they're going to know. Because I won't stop until I find the truth. Actually, I'm hoping you can help me."

Brennan looked startled. "How would I be able to help you?" As if she'd only just realized how her words sounded, she added, "Of course I will be happy to help any way I can, but I'm not sure how that's possible. It's always been my belief that Brandon was the one…and as I said, I was out of town."

Sasha stood. She reached into her bag and pulled out one of her cards. "I'm certain if you think about it, something will come to you. I still have your message to my mother the day before she was murdered. You were worried—you wanted to warn her about something. When you remember what that something was, call me. Please."

She placed her card on the desk and turned away from the woman's stunned gaze.

Sasha had a feeling she'd just shaken the lion's cage. A roar of a reaction would be coming.

Good. That was the point.

She rode the elevator down to the lobby and walked out of the building. She could almost feel Brennan's eyes on her as she climbed into her rental car.

All she had to do now was wait for the domino effect.

Chapter Ten

Luther Holcomb no longer lived in Winchester proper. After he retired four years ago, he divorced his wife and moved out into the woods in the middle of nowhere. He spent most of his time fishing or hunting.

Branch supposed a man who'd spent his life being a cop had the right to do whatever he wanted when he reached sixty-five without getting himself dead. Now, as Luther approached seventy, it seemed he rarely even came into town anymore.

Branch parked his truck and stared at the cabin directly in front of him. Was this what happened to a man who spent his life focused on catching criminals? Luther and his wife never had children and then after all those years they just walked away from so many decades invested in a marriage. Had they been living separate lives all along anyway? Branch knew lots of lawmen who did exactly that. The lives they led with the badge were the ones that consumed their existences. Their wives and kids had their own lives. Once in a while—like birthdays and holidays or graduations—those two lives intersected.

Branch didn't want that kind of life. Maybe it was the idea that he was barreling toward forty but he didn't want the family life he hoped to one day have to end up a casualty of his career. He wanted what his parents had. He wanted what his grandparents had shared.

He thought of Sasha and her daughter. What kind of life did they have together? Without the girl's dad in the picture? Her daughter—Brianne—had looked nothing like Branch had expected. He'd expected her to have her mother's dark hair and green eyes but she'd been blonde with blue eyes. Before he could stop his mind from going there, he imagined Sasha with some New York City hotshot. His gut tightened with envy.

A rap on the glass made him jump. His attention whipped in that direction to find Luther staring at him.

"You gonna sit in there all day?"

Branch couldn't believe he had allowed the old guy to sneak up on him. He opened the door and climbed out. "Hey, Luther, how are you doing?"

"Well, I'm still above ground, so that's always a good thing."

"Can't argue with that."

"Is this an official visit?" Luther eyed him speculatively.

"Kinda sorta." Branch closed the truck door and leaned against it. "Is that okay?"

Luther shrugged. "Sure. Why not? I just made a batch of shine if you're interested."

Branch shot him a grin. "I've had your shine before, Luther." He pressed a hand to his stomach. "I don't think I should go down that path today."

"When did they start making you guys so soft?" The older man laughed as he led the way into his house.

Branch followed, removing his hat at the door. "They like us to keep a clear head these days."

Luther grunted. "Is that supposed to make you better lawmen?"

"Presumably." Branch glanced around at the sparse furnishings and then at the bulletin board with its big calendar and all those crossed-out blocks. "You lining up your fishing calendar?"

"Oh, yeah." Luther poured himself a little shine in a mason jar and gestured to the seating area. "Sit. Tell me what you're up to, Mr. US Marshal."

Branch settled in the nearest chair. "Technically, I'm on vacation, but I'm helping a friend. You remember the Lenoir case?"

Luther collapsed into an ancient recliner. He knocked back a slug of his drink and then nodded. "How could I forget? It was an ugly mess. That poor little girl was shattered."

"That poor little girl is all grown up now," Branch commented, "and she wants to know what really happened that night."

Luther's gaze narrowed. "You think there was something wrong with the way I conducted the investigation?"

Branch had expected a bit of defensiveness. It was

human nature. "No, sir. I reviewed the reports and I think you did everything you could with what you had to work with at the time."

The tension in Luther's expression relaxed marginally and he indulged in another shot of homemade liquor, winced at the burn.

"I actually just have one question."

"What's that?" Luther set the mason jar down. "The scene was cut-and-dry. Easy to read. A blind man couldn't have missed the clues to what happened that night."

"Almost too easy," Branch noted. Then he asked his question. "Why didn't you put the little girl's statement in the file?"

Luther's eyebrows reared up. "You mean the one she came up with a week later?"

Branch didn't miss the guy's skepticism. "She insists she mentioned it the night her parents died but no one was listening."

"Let's take a minute and go over what I had," Luther suggested, "if you have the time."

"I have the time." Obviously Branch had struck a nerve. Not surprising. No lawman ever liked having one of his cases called into question.

"Brandon Lenoir got fired for drinking on the job. His blood alcohol level that night, by the way, was point one, well over the legal limit of impairment." Luther flared his hands. "Do the math. Taking into consideration his size, that means he had at least six beers or drinks in the couple of hours before he died. He didn't have a reputation for drinking, so I'm thinking that level of alcohol was unusual for him. People do crazy stuff when they're inebriated—especially someone not accustomed to being in that condition."

There was no denying that assessment. "So you're convinced Brandon Lenoir did this? No matter that he had no violent tendencies and from all reports loved his wife."

Luther shrugged. "Every killer starts somewhere. Many of them were never violent before their first kill. Sometimes people just snap. When he realized what he'd done, he killed himself."

"Why didn't he kill his daughter?" Branch countered. "He had to know where she was. If he wanted to kill his family, why leave her alive?"

Luther picked up the mason jar and had another swallow. "We explored the possibility that his wife was having an affair, but we found no evidence of infidelity—on either side."

"So basically they were a happy family with no serious problems. In fact, losing his job wasn't a major blow to their financial stability."

"Maybe it was a pride thing," Luther offered.

Branch wasn't buying it, particularly after last night. "You didn't answer my first question."

"The victim's advocate urged Mrs. Simmons to take the child to a psychiatrist. I did the same. She made an appointment immediately and the psychiatrist's report indicated the girl's story was something her mind conjured to make her feel better—a defense mechanism. What else was I supposed to do? Pursue a lead on a voice or voices that didn't exist?"

Branch couldn't deny the conundrum the man had faced. "You know my grandmother is still convinced Mr. Lenoir didn't kill his wife."

"She made her feelings known well enough." He laughed. "She complained louder than Mrs. Simmons."

"Did you consider why Mrs. Simmons kept so quiet? Is it possible she was afraid for her granddaughter's safety?"

This suggestion got the man's attention. "Did she tell her granddaughter that?"

Branch shook his head. "Nope, but someone broke into Mrs. Simmons's house last night and left a message for Sasha. *You were supposed to die that night.*"

"I guess word has gotten around that she's looking into the case. Some folks don't like the past being dug up."

"Unless they have something to hide, why all the fuss?"

"You got a point there, Marshal." He tossed back the last of his shine. "Let's talk off-the-record."

"This entire conversation is off-the-record," Branch reminded him. "I'm on vacation and anything I do or say is strictly coming from just me."

"No one really believed Brandon Lenoir would kill his wife, but stranger things have happened. The evidence was clear. There were powder burns on his hand. No indication of forced entry. No evidence of foul play anywhere on the property."

"But," Branch argued, "I'm guessing it was the

psychiatrist's conclusion that Sasha had made up the voices that convinced you to close the case?"

"If I have to pinpoint one thing, yeah. It was his report."

"Why isn't that report in the case file?" Seemed strange to Branch to leave out the primary reason for his conclusion.

"Mrs. Simmons didn't want any record of her granddaughter having emotional issues. I guess she was afraid the conclusion would haunt her in the future. I figure that honoring her wishes was the least I could do under the circumstances."

"Can I pass the psychiatrist's name on to Sasha? If he's still practicing she may want to meet with him."

"Sure. It was Dr. Bruce Farr. His office is across from the hospital. He doesn't see many patients anymore. He's some big-deal board member at the hospital these days."

Branch stood. "Thanks, Luther. I appreciate your help."

Luther pushed to his feet, gave Branch's hand a shake. "I'm not so sure I helped."

"If you think of anything else that might be useful, I would appreciate a call." Branch reached into his pocket and pulled out one of his cards.

"Sure thing." Luther took the card. "Bill called me. He wants to meet later to do this same thing."

Branch wasn't surprised. "It might be better if you don't mention I was here."

Luther grinned. "I never kiss and tell."

Branch was back on the main highway before his

cell service kicked in again. He pulled over to review a couple of text messages from Sasha. She had met with Leandra Brennan and learned very little. Chief Brannigan wanted to meet with her, so she was headed to city hall. Branch sent her a message explaining he'd met with Luther and intended to follow up with the shrink who had examined her, and then the coroner.

She promised to call him as soon as her meeting with Brannigan ended.

Branch drove back to town and took the turn that wound around by the hospital. Dr. Farr's office was a brick building directly across the street. Branch pulled into the small lot and climbed out. He settled his hat into place and walked to the entrance.

The door was locked. The office hours posted on the door showed Wednesday through Friday from one to four. There was an emergency contact number but Branch preferred catching the man in person to question him. He didn't want to give him a chance to prepare answers or to blow Branch off.

He moved on, heading to the veterinarian's office on Decherd Boulevard. The drive took only a few minutes. Burt Johnston had been the county coroner for about forty years. He also operated two large veterinarian offices. By trade the man was a veterinarian. Though he mostly oversaw the operations from a distance these days, folks still considered him the top vet in the area.

Didn't seem to matter to anyone that he also pronounced their deceased loved ones.

A technician waved Branch through. He found Burt in his office. Branch knocked and was summoned inside.

"Well, if it's not our celebrity US marshal. You chasing down another big mob element here in Winchester?"

Branch laughed. "No, I think we've cleared all that up."

Burt gestured to a chair. "What can I do for you today, Branch?"

"Tell me what you remember about the Lenoir case. Anything that stood out as a question for you?"

Burt shook his head. "It was a pretty straightforward situation." He shook his head again. "That poor child was the worst part. She was crying at the top of her lungs. Until we got her grandma there, it was a nightmare."

"Did you see anyone near the house that night who shouldn't have been there? Maybe someone who was there to see the show?"

Crime scenes were like car accidents—people often went out of their way to see.

"Not that I can recall. Two of Luther's boys got there first. Officers Kenyon and Lacon. When I arrived, Kenyon was in the front yard puking his guts out and Lacon was trying to calm the kid down."

"No neighbors or code scanners showed up?" Some folks listened to the police scanners and rushed to the scenes of crimes. The internet had made the uploading of photos and videos for titillation a way of life.

"The officers were there. I came next. I was already in the area when I received the call. The ambulance was right behind me and then Luther brought up the rear."

"As you know," Branch ventured, "Viola Simmons passed away and her granddaughter is in town settling her affairs. She has a lot of questions about what happened and she'd like to have answers to those questions while she's here. She's waited a long time to put this behind her. I've offered to help her find those answers."

"A lot of people weren't satisfied with the conclusions from that one, and frankly, I was one of them."

In Branch's opinion, having the coroner a bit skeptical was saying something. "Looking back, is there anything you would do differently today?"

He appeared to contemplate the question for a bit. "I would have sent a team through the woods a second time. They did a search that night but I would have done another at daylight. Luther didn't think it was necessary. He had the case nailed shut already. Personally I think the decision not to do a second search might have been a mistake. I'm convinced ignoring the little girl was one. I don't know that either issue would have changed anything, but better to be safe than sorry. Especially since the child said she heard voices besides her parents' in the house that night."

Branch frowned. "You certain about that? There are some who believe she never mentioned the voices until about a week later."

"You'd have to ask Luther to be certain, but I recall her saying something along those lines that night. Course, I was pretty focused on the bodies, but I'm reasonably sure I didn't hear wrong. In fact, I told Chief Brannigan the same thing this morning."

It appeared Brannigan was on the same track. No real surprise. "Thanks, Burt. I'll talk to Luther," Branch assured him.

The problem was, he already had.

Chapter Eleven

City hall looked basically the same as it had when Sasha was a child except for the metal detectors and the bag search. She'd come here with her grandmother once or twice after her parents died. Her grandmother had always gone into the chief's office while Sasha sat in a chair in the small lobby with the secretary or assistant to the chief.

She sat in a similar chair now. The upholstered chairs were different from the ones that had been here when she was a child but the polished tile floor was the same. The nondescript tan walls were the same. A couple more framed photos of officers who had lost their lives in the line of duty had been added to the one blue wall.

Sasha wasn't anticipating anything new in the chief's investigation of her parents' deaths. He'd only decided to reopen the case a few hours ago. Of course, there was the chance they had discovered some piece of evidence at her grandmother's house related to the break-in. Frankly, she was grateful for any support on the case. She hadn't expected to garner this much attention.

"Ms. Lenoir," the older woman behind the desk said, "the chief is ready to see you now."

Sasha stood and the door across the small room opened. The chief stepped out to greet her. "Thank you for coming, Ms. Lenoir."

Sasha thanked the secretary and entered the chief's office.

"Do you have some news for me, Chief?" She watched as he closed the door behind them.

"Actually, I have a few questions for you." He gestured to the pair of chairs in front of his desk. "Please, have a seat."

Sasha settled into one of the chairs and waited for the chief to do the same on the other side of the desk.

He leaned forward, scanned his notes. "I met with former chief of police Luther Holcomb and the county coroner, Burt Johnston. Both remembered the Lenoir case quite vividly. The trouble is I got conflicting stories about you from the two of them." Billy's gaze fixed on hers. "I know it's been a long time and that memories cloud with time, but this is one of those things that shouldn't be difficult to recall."

"How can I help, Chief?" Strange, Branch had the same two men on his list this morning. She wondered if he and Brannigan had run into each other.

"There seems to be some question as to when you actually mentioned hearing other voices—besides your parents'—in the house that night."

A frown tugged at her brow. She was surprised

by this particular question. "Chief Holcomb didn't include a statement from me in the official case file. He didn't feel my statement was credible. Are you saying you think that was a mistake?"

"Before we talk about my thoughts, did Chief Holcomb explain his reasoning for that decision?" Brannigan asked.

"There was some question as to why I didn't speak up earlier and the psychiatrist who evaluated me seemed to feel I was making up the whole story." Hurt and anger twisted inside her. She had been telling the truth. If everyone had listened to her then, maybe the investigation would have been conducted differently. Her grandmother had been so upset by Sasha's reactions to the sessions that she had refused to take Sasha back to see the man. At the time, Sasha had been glad. The doctor had made her feel strange, as if she were lying, and she had been telling the truth.

"I've tried to contact Dr. Farr, the psychiatrist who evaluated you, but he seems to be unavailable. The dilemma I have is that according to Burt Johnston, the coroner, you were talking about the other voices that very night, which directly conflicts with what Chief Holcomb says. Obviously, someone made a mistake. I just need to figure out which one is correct."

Sasha searched her memory of that night, tried to find a moment where she remembered speaking about the voices to someone amid the macabre activities happening around her. She remembered her parents' motionless bodies…the blood everywhere…

the anguished screams of her grandmother…the uniforms of the officers and the men from the ambulance. Sasha had felt as if she was in an odd bubble lingering all around the insanity but not quite inside it.

"Chief, parts of that night are a complete blur. I was in shock. Traumatized. If I was talking, I'm sure I said something about what I heard. The problem is, I can't actually remember speaking. If my grandmother was here…"

But she wasn't. Viola Simmons was gone. And with her, any information she had possessed about that horrendous night.

After so many years, how could Sasha hope to ever really know the truth? So many who might have known more were either dead or in bad health or simply no longer remembered.

Brannigan nodded, his expression filled with concern. "I've known Luther and Burt my whole life. They're both good men and neither would purposely misdirect a case. I would trust either one with my life. That said, one of them is wrong. Is there anyone else who would have been close enough to you and your family to know the details of that night?"

There was only one person. "Arlene Holloway. My grandmother and she were best friends. She might be able to help."

"I'll drop in on Mrs. Holloway. Thank you for coming by, Ms. Lenoir. Whatever you believe, I want to get to the bottom of this the same as you do."

"Thank you, Chief. That means a great deal to me."

As Sasha left the building, she noticed Leandra Brennan at the security desk in the lobby. The older woman spotted Sasha at about the same time and their gazes locked. Sasha held her gaze until her mother's old friend Lenny looked away. What kind of friend withheld potential information that might be able to cast new light on an old tragedy?

"The chief's office is directly that way, ma'am."

Sasha turned, walking backward and watching the Brennan woman as she strode toward the chief's office. Funny, there was no statement in the case file from her mother's best friend. Sasha wasn't a cop or a private investigator, but she could not see how that was right under any circumstances. Anyone close to her parents should have been interviewed. It simply didn't make sense. Brennan had insisted that she was out of town and nothing she knew was relevant, and apparently Chief Holcomb had taken her at her word.

A huge mistake, in Sasha's opinion. The woman was definitely hiding something.

Outside, she stood on the sidewalk and stared at the fading afternoon sun. She had been back in Winchester since Thursday evening—mere hours after she received the call about her grandmother. Friday Rey had taken care of all the funeral arrangements and Sasha had gone through photo albums and boxes of her grandmother's stored treasures. It wasn't until sometime Saturday that the reality sunk in. Her grandmother was dead.

Sasha climbed into her rental and drove the short distance to the cemetery. She hadn't been back there since the burial on Sunday. Right now she just needed to go back. To be near her grandmother.

She drove to the section of the cemetery where the family plot was and parked. The breeze kicked up and she shivered. Growing up, she'd never liked cemeteries. She would never forget watching her parents' caskets lowered into the cold ground.

A part of her had vanished that day. She hadn't seen that little girl since.

She walked over to the family plot, which was quite large. Simmonses had been buried here for several generations. Sasha sat down on the bench her grandmother had had installed near her parents' graves. The double headstone sat right next to the double one for her grandparents.

There was still enough space in the plot right next to her parents' for another double headstone. Would she need a double? She hadn't even come close to the altar or even moving in with a significant other.

It was just she and Brianne.

Sasha studied the date on the headstone that belonged to her parents. She suspected that her grandmother had only buried them next to each other for Sasha's benefit. Looking back, what mother who actually believed a man had killed her daughter would want him buried in the family plot for any reason— even to appease her nine-year-old granddaughter?

Had Viola really believed the official conclusions?

So many aspects of the tragedy were contradictory. So many pieces didn't properly fit into place.

But was she looking for a reason to believe her

father was innocent? Had someone else been doing the same thing when they broke into her house and left that note?

Now she was really grasping at straws. She reminded herself that Branch Holloway and Billy Brannigan would not be poking around in the case unless they suspected something was amiss.

Several headstones away, she noted a blonde woman wearing a dark sweater. Arms hugged tightly around her slim body, she stood staring down at a wide granite marker. Sasha watched her for a moment, sensing she should recognize her. The breeze pushed the hair back from her cheek and Sasha realized who she was. Rowan DuPont, the undertaker's daughter. She'd buried her father in this cemetery barely a week ago. Like Sasha, she was alone now—except Sasha had her daughter. But the last of her ancestors were gone. Somehow the realization made the loss all the more difficult.

She checked her cell. Nothing from Branch yet. She should go back to the house and look around some more. The memories had really been coming inside that old house, and as difficult as it was to be there, this—*venture*—was about revisiting the past. More often than not the truth was not comfortable.

Discomfort she was prepared for.

Sasha called her daughter as she walked back to her car. There were more questions about Branch and more teasing. Deep down it pleased Sasha that her daughter thought he was good-looking. She'd had a great day at school and only had one more test this week. She could leave for Winchester tomorrow afternoon and spend the rest of the week. Sasha managed to talk her out of that one. She promised to text good-night.

When the call ended Sasha was halfway across town before she remembered to text Branch with her change of plans. She had promised to keep him informed of her whereabouts. Not that she was opposed to doing so; she'd simply forgotten. After her late-night visitor, he was right about keeping in touch. When she made the turn onto the long narrow driveway, she braked long enough to send the text. Then she rolled the quarter of a mile to her childhood home.

This late in the afternoon it was almost dark on the porch. Sasha unlocked the front door and flipped on a light. She'd spent a lot of time in her mother's office when she was here before. No need to pilfer around in there today.

She climbed the stairs, turning on lights, watching the dust motes float through the air. Bypassing her own room, she walked into her parents' room. This time, rather than look through drawers, she went to the closet and started digging through pockets and bags. Her mother had owned a dozen or more handbags. Sasha fished through each one and found nothing. She ran her hands into each pocket on each pair of pants and blouse or dress. Not one thing. Not a scrap of paper, a business card or even a piece of lint.

Viola had taken most all her daughter's jewelry, except the pearls, to her house and put it away for Sasha, so there was nothing in the jewelry box. That left only one unexplored space—the bathroom. Of course, the original investigation had checked for drugs and anything that might be considered contraband.

Sasha checked each item in the bathroom. Every bottle of makeup, stick of deodorant and jar of liquid soap. There was nothing that should not be there. Nothing unexpected. She turned toward the door, her gaze landing on the tissue box on the back of the toilet. No point leaving a single stone unturned.

She picked up the box and pulled out tissue after tissue, allowing them to fall onto the closed toilet seat. Obviously she was losing it. Rolling her eyes, she started to put the box back and then she noticed the blue on the white tissues. Sasha picked up the one on top.

Major structural flaws.

She dragged another from the box. It, too, was marred with blue ink.

Material will be stressed beyond its strength.

Then another. *Monumental failure at some point in the future.*

And the next. *Don't know what to do.*

Sasha's heart was thundering by the time she reached the last tissue in the box.

Can't tell Brandon.

She wasn't sure what this meant but it had to be important. Why else would her mother hide the notes in the bathroom tissue box?

Sasha could imagine her mother sitting alone in

this bathroom, worried and afraid, and making notes to herself…or to anyone who might find them.

Cold seeped into Sasha's bones. The idea of her mother being afraid twisted her heart.

She pulled her cell from her pocket and checked her screen. Why hadn't Branch responded to her text?

A red exclamation answered the question. Message failed to send.

A scan of the top of the screen explained why. No service.

She hit Try Again with the same result.

"Well, damn." Maybe the service would be better outside. She shoved the tissues back into the box and stowed it under her arm.

The house was utterly silent. No humming refrigerator sound. No soft purr of the heating or cooling systems. No ticking clock. So when a creak splintered the air Sasha froze in her tracks.

There was no gun in the house. No weapons that she was aware of… Maybe a knife in the kitchen.

But she wasn't in the kitchen.

Then she remembered the security system. She rushed to her father's side of the bed and dragged the baseball bat from under the skirt.

Her heart pounding, Sasha placed the box of tissues on the nightstand and gripped the bat with both hands. Moving slowly in hopes of not hitting a squeaky spot in the floor, she eased out of her parents' room. She made it to the hall without a sound. Downstairs the intruder wasn't so careful. He had just entered the kitchen.

Could it be the same guy from last night?

She was halfway down the staircase when the tread beneath her right foot creaked.

Sasha froze.

Silence seemed to explode all around her and yet there was utter stillness, utter quiet. It was the blood roaring through her veins that sounded like an explosion.

The crash of the back door banking off the siding jolted her into motion once more. Sasha ran for the kitchen. As she reached the door that stood wide open, she spotted a male in dark clothes and a dark cap disappearing into the woods.

She hesitated for only a moment. Long enough to hit Try Again and then to send Branch another text.

Intruder!

Sasha shoved her phone into her pocket and ran for the woods, the bat held at the ready. "Stop!" she shouted.

When she reached the woods she scanned the trees, caught a glimpse of a dark shape fading into the shadows.

She hurried in that direction. "Hey! What do you want?"

Her voice reverberated around her, bouncing off the trees.

She ran until she stopped seeing glimpses of the fleeing man. Then she skidded to a stop.

Her breath heaving in and out of her lungs, she surveyed the gloom. Nothing. And it was so damned quiet. Frustrated and feeling completely ridiculous, she started to turn around. Branch would be furious when he found out what she'd done. She'd run toward the trouble rather than away.

Not smart, Sasha. Even if she did have her father's baseball bat.

The corner of something rustic and out of place captured her attention.

Wood and metal.

The shack. Sasha cut through the dense underbrush, following a now hidden path that she knew by heart.

Her jaw dropped as she stared at the dilapidated structure. The shack was maybe eight feet by ten and perhaps seven feet tall. Her father had told her it was at least a hundred years old when she was a little girl.

This had been her playhouse by the time she was seven years old and knew how to sneak through the woods without her mother or her grandmother knowing she'd disappeared. She had come here nearly every day.

She reached for the old door. It wasn't a real door. Just a bunch of boards nailed together and hung on hinges. The wood was rotting around the edges of the door and the hinges squeaked when she pulled it open. Wood banged against wood as the door plopped against the exterior of the shack.

Inside she blinked to hasten the adjustment of her eyes. There were cobwebs and dust. Lots of dust like in the house.

Against the far wall was a blanket. A discarded soft-drink can and a bit of other food trash. Had someone been staying here?

No, wait. The layer of dust on everything suggested no one had been here in a very long time.

Sasha stepped into the small space and picked up a potato chip bag. She searched until she found the expiration date: one year after her parents died.

Whoever had been staying in here could very well have been here when her parents were murdered.

Why had no one checked this shack?

The more she learned about the investigation the more convinced she became that the chief of police at the time had not wanted to unravel the facts. Suddenly aware that she was contaminating a potential crime scene, she eased out of the shack. Bat gripped firmly in her hands, she surveyed the woods around her. Clear. She headed back toward the house. She'd just passed the tree line when a hand snagged her arm.

Sasha tried to swing the bat, but he held her tight.

Her scream rent the air.

Chapter Twelve

Branch.

It was only Branch.

Sasha dragged in a breath, tried to calm her racing heart.

"What the hell happened?" He glanced around the overgrown yard. "There was an intruder? *Here?*"

She had made it back to the yard. Branch had obviously just arrived and spotted her barreling out of the woods. The other man—person—was gone. "There was someone in the house with me. When he heard me he ran. I…" She moistened her lips, braced for his disapproval. "I followed him into the woods, but I lost him near the shack."

Branch visibly restrained his frustration. She watched the struggle play out on his face. "Did you get a look at his face?"

She shook her head. "He wore dark clothes and a skullcap."

"How tall was he?"

"Average." She shrugged. "Medium build, maybe a little on the thin side."

Her knees were slightly weak now with the receding adrenaline. She steadied herself and braced for whatever he had to say next. No doubt a lecture on common sense or something along those lines.

He looked away for a moment, his hands planted on his hips. She had a feeling he had planted them there to prevent shaking her. Now that she thought about it, maybe she needed to be shaken. She had come here—to this desolate place—alone. After last night she should have known better.

She hadn't been thinking. Sasha was accustomed to being strong and fearless. This sort of uncertainty was not the norm for her.

"What's this about a shack?"

So maybe she was going to skate through this without a raking over the coals from Branch. "When I was a kid I played there. My father said the shack was really old, like a century old or more. It looks as if someone was staying in there."

He frowned. "In the shack?"

She shook her head, then nodded. She wasn't making sense. "Not today, but back when the murders happened. Come this way—I'll show you."

He hesitated at first but then he relented and started forward with her.

"Point the way," he said, "and stay behind me."

"Yes, sir." She gave him a little salute. He shot her a look that said he was not playing.

Sasha guided him back to the shack with only one wrong turn. When she'd stumbled upon it a little while ago she'd been chasing the intruder and she hadn't been thinking. It had been twenty-seven years since she'd visited this shack.

She spotted a flash of rusty metal roof to their left. "There it is."

They moved through the overgrowth of saplings and brush until they were standing beside it. The squatty primitive structure looked smaller with Branch looming nearby.

"Did you go inside?" he asked.

"Yes. For a moment."

He pulled the door open and used his cell as a flashlight to illuminate the interior. It was darker now, the setting sun withdrawing its feeble reach through the dense trees.

There was the blanket she'd seen and the food refuse.

"The chip bag shows an expiration date the year of my parents' deaths." She pointed to the bag, now wishing she hadn't walked inside. "It's possible someone was staying here when my parents were murdered. There could be prints or other evidence."

Branch leaned inside, surveyed the space more closely with the aid of the flashlight app. "The dust on the floor looks undisturbed before today."

Yes, she had made a mistake. "Whatever's in here could still be useful, though, right?"

Her desperation was showing. No one hated that kind of slip more than her.

"It could. Absolutely." He withdrew his upper body from the shack and put through a call on his cell.

"Hey, Billy, we have a new development over at the Lenoir property."

While Branch explained recent events to the chief of police, Sasha surveyed the woods, hoping she might spot the man who had sneaked into the house. He had to have seen her car parked in front of it. If he knew she was there, why try sneaking in? Had he hoped to get a drop on her? He hadn't appeared to be armed—or even after her, for that matter. He'd run away. Was he only watching her? Or was he like her, searching for something that would lead to the truth?

"I wasn't able to talk to that shrink," Branch said, drawing her attention back to him. He propped one shoulder against the side of the shack to wait. "He apparently doesn't operate by his posted business hours."

"Brannigan couldn't reach him either."

There was something else she'd forgotten: to brief him on her meeting with Brannigan. They would have gotten around to it eventually, she felt confident. At his prompting, she explained the differing statements from Holcomb and Johnston as well as the idea that Brannigan seemed intent on getting to the bottom of the discrepancy.

"Unfortunately my memory of events after I came out of the closet that night is not reliable." She chewed at her lip and considered whether there was more she should be telling him. "And I saw Leandra Brennan going to the chief's office as I was leaving."

"Burt told me the same thing about that night,"

Branch said. "He feels Luther closed the case too quickly. Burt wasn't happy with the limited search around the property or the fact that Luther blew off your assertions. But then, Burt is the coroner. He's not a detective. Still, I agree with him. This—" he hitched his head toward the shack "—is a perfect example of why a more thorough and expansive search should have taken place that night. Nothing may come of this, but it should have been done back then."

Sasha didn't remember Luther Holcomb well enough to reach any sort of conclusion on this news, so she asked, "Is there any chance Holcomb was part of the cover-up?"

Branch's lips formed a grim line for a long moment before he spoke. "I don't think so. There have never been any rumors about his work or about him. He had a stellar reputation when he was chief and no one has suggested otherwise. Course, I was gone for a lot of years. I'll talk to Billy and see what he thinks. Billy worked with him until he retired four years ago. If we have reason to be concerned about his actions in the investigation, Billy will know."

Sasha felt suddenly immensely tired.

For twenty-seven years she had been waiting for the truth about what happened to her parents. She had put off pushing for that truth as long as her grandmother was alive because it was too painful for her. She had told Sasha this only once when, at sixteen, Sasha had demanded she hire a private investigator. When Viola had tearfully begged for Sasha to put that part of the past behind her once and for all, she'd had no choice. She could not bear to hurt her grandmother.

Now she understood a little of what her grandmother did not want to face. It was overwhelming and frustrating and painful all at the same time. Those in law enforcement—like Branch—trying to help were so incredibly important to the probability of success. Now the chief of police and the coroner were involved. It was finally, really happening, and Sasha was drowning in all those overpowering emotions.

"We should walk back to the house," Branch offered. "Or Billy's officers will be swarming the woods after us."

Over the next hour Brannigan arrived and was escorted to the shack by Branch, and then the forensics unit was called. The part that made the chief of police so happy was the fact that the intruder hadn't appeared to be wearing any gloves. Until he asked, Sasha hadn't considered whether the man had or not, but when her mind replayed him running away, his hands were bare.

Maybe this was the break they needed.

EVENING HAD GIVEN way to night and it was well after dark when Branch insisted on driving her home.

"There's nothing else we can do here," he told her.

He was right, except a part of her wanted to stay as long as there was still activity going on, but she relented. "There's something in the house I need to grab first."

Branch followed her to the back door. She retrieved the box of tissues and declared she was ready to go. Branch didn't question the move. During the drive she thought of the things her mother had written on the tissues. Had she been brainstorming? Trying to work out a path to take some sort of action? Had she hoped that someone would find her notes?

How could they possibly?

By the time they reached Branch's house, Sasha felt agitated. Had her mother been in some sort of trouble? Who had known? Why hadn't someone helped her? Was this why the woman who had been her best friend pretended she knew nothing? Had she abandoned Sasha's mother when she needed her most? What had her father known? Was this situation related to his work at a major construction company?

Sasha closed her eyes for a moment. How in the world could she possibly find the answers after all these years?

"You okay?"

She opened her eyes and turned to Branch. They were parked in his driveway and he sat behind the wheel watching her.

"I'm not sure." She stared forward. "I'm really not sure at all."

"Let's go inside, have a bite to eat and tackle this one piece at a time. I think you're feeling inundated because of all the questions and all the possibilities."

He was right. She nodded. "Okay."

On the porch, she held tight to her box of tissues

while Branch unlocked his front door. He flipped on the lights and inhaled deeply. "You smell that?"

Sasha stepped inside and took a deep breath. "I do. Smells like roast and fresh-baked bread."

He shoved the door closed, gave the lock a twist. "My grandmother has been here. She was afraid I wouldn't feed you right."

Sasha had to smile. "Well, it smells heavenly."

They followed the aroma into the kitchen. Arlene had left a note on the island.

Dinner is in the oven. Make sure she eats.

Sasha laughed out loud then. "I think we can make that happen."

"I'll get a couple of beers," Branch offered.

"I'll check the oven." Sasha left her bag and her box of tissues on a chair.

Branch had a nice house. It wasn't a new build but it was recently renovated. His kitchen was particularly stylish with modern appliances. The casserole dish in the oven was covered in aluminum foil. Sasha settled it on the stovetop and removed the foil. Potatoes and carrots and a roast. Looked as good as it smelled. On the counter was a basket filled with freshly made rolls.

Two bottles of beer landed on the counter then and Branch grabbed bowls and spoons. They filled their bowls and settled around the island. The roast tasted just as amazing as it smelled. The rolls melted on the tongue and the beer was the perfect contrast to all the smooth, rich tastes and textures.

When Sasha couldn't eat another bite, she pushed her bowl away. "Your grandmother is an amazing cook."

"She is." Branch pushed his bowl away, too. "She spoils me."

"I suspect this is something else you'll miss if you move to Nashville."

He nodded. "No doubt. Course, there's always Sundays. My grandmother feeds everyone on Sundays. The whole Holloway crew."

Sasha needed to start traditions like that. She and her daughter only had a couple. Traditions, even small ones, were important to future bonding. One day her daughter would be all grown up and have a family of her own. The thought terrified Sasha. She glanced at Branch, who was putting their bowls into the dishwasher.

This was another past wrong that Sasha had to make right. Soon. Very soon.

"I asked Billy if he could share any information about his interview with Leandra Brennan. He couldn't."

Sasha paused in her work covering the leftover roast. "But he did call her into his office about the investigation."

Branch nodded. "He also called her a hostile witness, so she didn't come in voluntarily."

Sasha shook her head. "I just want to know the story there. Arlene has no idea?"

"I asked her if she remembered any issues and

she didn't. She says your mom and Brennan weren't really that close."

Surprised, Sasha started to question him further but she suddenly remembered the box of tissues. "There's something I need to show you."

She retrieved the box of tissues and went back to the island. Claiming a stool, she placed the box on the counter.

"I think we might need another beer," he said with a curious glance at the box.

"Good idea."

He grabbed two bottles from the fridge and joined her at the island.

"I searched everything in my parents' bedroom. As I was finishing up, I realized this was the one place I hadn't looked." She tapped the box. "So I pulled the tissues out, thinking something might be hidden inside—I guess I've watched too many movies. At any rate, this is what I found."

She spread the tissues with blue ink across the counter.

Major structural flaws.

Material will be stressed beyond its strength.

Monumental failure at some point in the future.

Don't know what to do.

Sasha's heart started that painful squeezing again when she read the last one.

Can't tell Brandon.

"You're certain this is your mother's handwriting?"

Sasha nodded. "Positive."

"Then it looks like we have ourselves a starting place."

Sasha met his gaze. "You think the murders were related to one or the other's work?"

"I was leaning in that direction already, but this makes it pretty clear." He searched her gaze. "Your mother was responsible for approving plans and architectural drawings for every building that was constructed in this county for as long as she held the position. Any issues with the plans would have been flagged by her office. These—" he tapped the counter near the tissues "—are the sorts of issues developers don't want to hear about."

"Are you saying someone could have wanted to stop her from doing her job?"

He nodded. "That's exactly what I'm saying."

Sasha put a hand over her mouth so he wouldn't see her lips trembling.

"I'm sorry. I didn't mean that to sound so callous."

"No." She put her hand over his, almost jumped at the soft zing that sparked between them. "You've been nothing but helpful and a great friend. I couldn't have done this without you, Branch."

With his free hand he reached up and stroked her cheek with the tips of his fingers. Warmth spread through her. "I'm grateful for the opportunity to do the right thing." He let his hand fall away but didn't draw from her touch. "I shouldn't have left the way I did."

She frowned, not understanding what he meant. Then she realized he was talking about the morning after their one-night stand. She held her hands up, withdrawing contact. "We were young. It was…"

"Thoughtless," he argued. "I had to be back in Chicago but I should have delayed my flight and at least spent some time with you."

If either of them had anything to be sorry for, it was her, but she couldn't bring herself to confess. She just couldn't go there right now. She needed his help. How selfish was that?

"You didn't do anything wrong, Branch."

He gave her a nod. "We can agree to disagree. For now, let's start a list of possible suspects."

She blinked. Okay, so they were back on the case now. Good. "You go first."

"Leandra Brennan."

Sasha was surprised. "Really?"

He gave an affirming nod. "She still works for the same developer. One of the largest, most powerful ones in the Southeast."

"Okay."

He came up with paper and a pen and they started their list.

She liked being shoulder to shoulder with him as they jotted down the names. She liked his smile and the sound of his voice.

She liked everything about him, actually.

Her daughter was right. He was hot.

Slow it down, Sash.

Right now she could without question say that Branch was a really good friend. Whatever happened after this, it had to be a slow build toward total honesty…and hopefully forgiveness.

She would need his when he had the whole truth.

Chapter Thirteen

Wednesday, March 27

Branch had just poured the coffee when Sasha appeared in the kitchen. He'd had a hard time sleeping last night, as much because she was sleeping in his bed as because of the case.

"Morning." He set a mug of steaming brew on the counter in front of her. "I hope you slept well." Toast popped up in the toaster.

"I did." She picked up the mug, cradled it in both hands. "Actually, I slept better than I have since I arrived." She sipped her coffee.

"I'm glad." He turned his own cup up to prevent saying more. He hoped she felt safe in his home… in his *bed*. He wanted her to feel safe with him. "I thought we could talk about the list over some toast."

They hadn't gotten very far on their list last night. *Brennan* was the only name scribbled there so far. He'd been toying with a few others. He'd already put in a call to Billy about pulling records to find out what planned developments Sasha's mother had been working on the final year of her life. There would hopefully be notes in the records if any of the developers or builders had given her any trouble or if any issues had cropped up with the properties during construction or later on.

"Toast would be perfect."

He slathered butter on both pieces, placed each on a small plate and offered one to her. "Jelly?"

"No, thanks." She nibbled a bite. "Perfect."

He devoured his in a few bites, washed it down with coffee.

"I've been thinking about Leandra Brennan." Sasha dabbed her lips with a napkin. "I sent a text to Rey—you know Audrey Anderson at the newspaper."

He nodded. "I know her, yes." Audrey Anderson had been accidentally instrumental in the resuscitation of his wounded career. The remains buried in the basement of her newspaper had set off shock waves from here to Chicago. Not to mention, a highly sought after federal witness had been hiding amid the Mennonite community in Franklin County and Audrey had helped shake him loose.

"I realized that Brennan is about the same age my mother would be if she were still alive," Sasha explained, "so I asked Rey to check her extensive resources to see if the two attended school together. Well, you know Rey—thorough is her middle name. She sent me a very long text this morning. The two went to school together from kindergarten through high school graduation. They were accepted into the same college from which they both graduated, and they were married the same summer—they were each other's maid and matron of honor."

Branch had never been married or even engaged, but even he understood the maid and matron of honor thing was a big deal. "So they were *really* close."

Sasha nodded. "*Really* close. The big difference was children. Mother and Daddy had me a few years after they were married. Brennan didn't have her first child until the year my parents were murdered. She had a son that fall and then another one two years later. The thing is, I couldn't understand why I didn't really remember her. You would think friends that close would have done more than have the occasional lunch together. I would expect shopping sprees, picnics and barbecues, and maybe even family vacations, but I don't recall anything like that involving Brennan."

"You should ask Arlene," Branch offered. "Maybe there's more to the story that she didn't mention."

"There has to be. It's too strange." She picked up her mug again. "I mentioned to Rey that the murders might have been related to trouble with one or both of my parents' workplaces, so she did a little digging there, too." Sasha touched the screen of her phone, forcing it to light up. "On my mother's side there were several small issues with zoning and site developments, as well as architectural review setbacks, but only a few were noteworthy. The big-box store that opened on the boulevard was one. The drama played out in the courtroom before an agreement was reached. The extension at the auto manufacturer facility created a little commotion in the community. There was some question as to whether the adjoining property was properly zoned. But it was the William Richards Stadium that generated the most buzz. Apparently my mother was embroiled in a major battle over design issues that failed to meet code. According to Rey, it got really ugly in the media and in the city meetings."

"That was the year before, though, right?" Branch remembered his father commenting that the stadium might not happen because of some sort of design flaws.

"It was."

Branch added the stadium to their list. "We can get the developers' names for both the stadium and the big-box store. Anything on your dad's side?"

"There was some issue with the hospital." She shrugged. "The construction company he worked for was contracted to complete some part of the project and then midway into the project they pulled out. Rey said her father did an editorial piece on the disagreement but otherwise there was no mention of the trouble in the papers. Whatever happened, it was settled fairly quietly."

"The hospital would be a Packard project. Brennan works for Packard." Now, there was an interesting connection. "I almost hate to say it out loud, but I can see Packard being involved with murder." Branch surprised himself with the announcement. Maybe it was because his father despised the man,

Jarvis Packard. Whatever the case, Branch couldn't help seeing him as a scumbag—a rich one, but a scumbag nonetheless.

"Beyond the connection with Brennan, why would you feel so strongly about Packard? Is there something else I should know?"

"Something my father said on several occasions when I was a kid." He should ask him about it. "He said a man was only as good as his word and Jarvis Packard's word was as worthless as sand in the desert."

Sasha nodded. "That's fairly worthless."

Branch laughed. "In my father's opinion, anyway."

Their gazes caught and for a long moment they looked at each other. It was one of those moments when you didn't know whether to speak or to act. Either one seemed like a risk to what came next, and yet the urge to do the latter was nearly overwhelming. Branch went with the former.

"This is not the time, I get that, but I want to kiss you more than I've wanted to do anything in a very long time."

For another endless second she only stared at him. Then she smiled. "I'm having trouble with that, too. I'm sure we shouldn't—"

Before she could say more, he leaned across the counter and kissed her. She tasted of coffee and felt like silk. He hesitated, their lips still touching, and when she didn't pull away he deepened the kiss. He wanted to walk around this damned island and pull her into his arms. He wanted to carry her to his bed and make love to her. He wanted to do it the right way this time.

A cell rattled against the counter with a lively tune and Sasha drew away. "That's my daughter. I have to take this."

She rushed away, but not before Branch saw her touch her lips and draw in a sharp breath. He wondered if her lips were on fire the way his were or if her heart was pounding as his was. He should have gone after her all those years ago. He'd never wanted anyone the way he did Sasha and he'd kept it to himself all this time. For no other reason than so he could focus on his career, and just maybe there had been a little fear involved.

His dad and his grandmother had warned him often that there were more important things in life than one's career. He'd had to learn that the hard way.

When he'd shaken off the lingering lust, he made a call to Billy and brought him up to speed on what he and Sasha were thinking.

"I can do some checking. See if Packard has had any issues since then. Any lawsuits or code violations. You know," the chief of police pointed out, "it's always easy to finger the bully—the one everybody expects to be bad. But it's not always the bully who does the bad stuff."

Branch shut off the coffee maker and rinsed the carafe as the man spoke. "You've been here all these years and I've been out of the picture until recently. If we're putting the number one pushy developer aside for the moment, who's your runner-up?"

"Keegan and Roark, they built the stadium. They wanted in on the hospital deal—according to my daddy. They intended to make a huge donation and have a wing named after them, but Packard wouldn't have it. He didn't want their money. Some long-ago bad blood, the way I hear it."

Branch had a funny feeling Billy was feeding him all this information for a reason. "Not that I don't appreciate the heads-up," he confessed, "but I have to say, I'm surprised you're sharing all this with me, Chief. Is there something I should be reading between the lines?"

A few seconds of silence elapsed. "This is all speculation, Branch. I don't have a speck of evidence. I can't exactly investigate a problem that doesn't exist. As you well know, that's not the way it works in law enforcement. Someone has to break the law before I can investigate. On the other hand, a guy working off-the-record—on vacation, let's say—can poke around to his heart's desire as long as he doesn't break any laws."

Someone had warned Billy to back off.

"I guess there are folks who don't like to see the city waste resources on a cold case."

"Especially when the fingerprints found in a certain shack lead to a man who went missing twenty-seven years ago and eventually ended up as a long-term resident in a psychiatric facility."

Branch's instincts perked up. Oh, he remembered the case. "Are we talking about Packard's son Devlin?"

"Bingo."

That was one case Branch doubted anyone would forget. Devlin Packard had come home on spring break the same year Sasha's parents died. Before the week's end, he had abruptly disappeared. Months later, when he was found, the guy was strung out on drugs. The word was he never recovered. "Devlin would be what? About forty-seven or -eight now? The last I heard, he was still in an assisted living facility of some sort."

"He was, until he walked out about three days ago. No one has seen him since."

Tension coiled inside Branch. "Was he the one staying in the shack when the Lenoirs were murdered?"

"He's been in there at some point in the past and I'm guessing he was the one in the Lenoir house when Sasha was there. Maybe even in the Simmons house the other night. The timing would fit."

"Is he dangerous?" Worry gnawed at Branch's gut.

"No violent tendencies. Always the ideal patient. Then he just ups and walks out. His daddy has a whole posse of his security minions out looking for him."

Sasha walked back into the kitchen. Branch would have to find a way to convince her to stay close, particularly after this news.

Good luck with that.

"Anything else?" Branch asked. Sasha had her handbag. Obviously she was ready to go. The second intruder had done little to deter her. But then, he couldn't blame her. She had waited a long time for the truth.

"That's it for now. Watch your step, Branch. Something is wrong with this case and I can't quite put my finger on it. I had no idea so much had been swept under the rug. By the way, thanks for the heads-up on Leandra Brennan. She didn't have much to say but she knows plenty. I'll be watching her. I'm hoping when she realizes I'm not pushing this case back into a drawer, she'll come around."

"I'll touch base with you later today." Branch severed the connection and settled his full attention on Sasha. "We may have an ID on the intruder."

"That's great."

He briefed her on the latest from Brannigan. The news only seemed to create more questions rather than provide answers. Branch was feeling the same rising tension.

One step forward, two steps back.

"Why would Packard's son have been staying in the shack?"

Branch mentally ran through a couple of scenarios. "It's possible he was involved with a drug dealer on that side of town and happened upon the shack by accident. It was empty, so he made himself a home. I remember my parents talking about his disappearance. The rumor was he had some kind of breakdown."

"But you said he had shown no violent tendencies, so it's not likely that he committed the murders."

"There's always a first time," Branch countered.

"The truth is, if he went over the edge in some sort of psychotic break, he may have done some very violent things and have no recall of the events. This would explain why Packard has kept him locked away all this time."

Even as Branch said the words, he thought of Billy's suggestion that the bad guy was not always the obvious bully. But maybe this time the glaringly obvious bully was the bad guy. Sometimes bad guys liked hiding in plain sight. The boldness of the move gave them a sense of power.

Sasha squared her shoulders. "I intend to track down Dr. Farr today. I want to know why he concluded that I made up the voices. I want to know what else he said in his report. In fact, I believe I have the right to demand a copy of his report."

Branch thought of her daughter and realized that Sasha was the only family the girl had left since her dad was not in the picture. "I'm not sure you going off on your own is such a good idea, Sasha. Your daughter is counting on you to come back home when this is over. Any risk you take is a risk to her."

Sasha held up her hands. "I'm a good mother, Branch. I always consider my daughter's needs first." When he would have tried to explain himself, she added, "I am perfectly capable of driving across town to Dr. Farr's office on my own. I've done pretty well so far."

The woman lived in a major metropolitan area. She was accustomed to taking care of herself in far more risky environments than this one simply due to the nature of her work. She obviously knew how to handle herself. But they were just getting started with this case and a media-binging pop star with a bad attitude was vastly different from a cold-blooded killer. Things could escalate quickly.

"I let you talk me into going our separate ways yesterday and you got into a dicey situation," he reminded her. "I don't think we should go down that same path again today. And for the record, I'm certain you're a fantastic mother and very capable."

"Okay." Sasha exhaled a big breath. "Let's compromise. I'll track down the shrink while you do whatever it is you need to do, and then we'll meet up to see what we have." Before he could utter his protest, she urged, "I will go only to the man's office and to the hospital looking for him. Nowhere else."

"No going back to your old home place or to your grandmother's house without me. Basically no going anywhere you might end up alone and cornered."

"You have my word."

He nodded. "All right, but I want to hear from you every half hour."

She rolled her eyes. "Fine. And what about you? What will you be doing?"

"I'm going to the office where your mother worked and see how difficult it's going to be to get into their archives. Most of the files are public record, so we'll see."

"You think it was Packard, don't you?"

The lady was far too perceptive.

"I think Packard probably has more motive than

anyone else simply because of the sheer number of projects he was and is involved with."

"Whoever was responsible," she said, her voice overly quiet, "he had something to hide. Something my mother knew about. But there haven't been any epic fails of structures or roads or anything like that, which seems to negate the entire idea."

"Maybe he's gotten lucky until now. The trouble might be just around the corner or coming in the next decade. But we know there was something. Something big enough to kill for. And if he killed once to keep his secret, he won't hesitate to kill again."

She was backing away from him before he could talk himself out of allowing her out of his sight. "We'll catch up as soon as I've spoken to Dr. Farr."

Branch grabbed his keys and his hat. "I'll follow up with Brennan while I'm at it."

She glanced at him, clearly surprised by that move.

"Now that the chief of police has rattled that cage," he explained, "I'm hoping she'll be a little more co-operative."

Billy's hands had been tied to some degree. Branch didn't have that trouble.

"She has the answers we need," Sasha insisted. "I'm certain of it."

One way or another Branch intended to find out.

Chapter Fourteen

Sasha met Rey at the diner for an early lunch. The toast she'd had with Branch was long gone. A Cobb salad was just the ticket. She decided to forego the dressing and just enjoy the rich ingredients and a glass of sweet iced tea with lemon in honor of her grandmother. Viola Simmons had loved sweet tea.

"I did some additional research on Devlin," Rey said. She stabbed a forkful of her greens. "He's a resident at Mountain View, a private resort-like facility in Sewanee. No hardship there, I can tell you. I did a piece on the services they provide. Only the very best. I'm surprised he walked out of such a posh environment. Mountain View is known for top-notch patient care."

"Do you know his diagnosis?" Rey was good at ferreting out information. However, Sasha wasn't sure if what she was asking with that question was something she could learn without doing so via some illegal avenue. There were some things even the best investigative reporter couldn't uncover. The HIPAA

Law was generally a brick wall when it came to protecting the privacy rights of patients.

"A distant cousin who visits him occasionally tells me it's schizophrenia and drug addiction. He can't stay on the prescribed meds and off the non-prescribed ones, so he can't stay healthy, thus the long-term residency. He long ago made the choice to become a permanent resident rather than deal with life outside those insulating walls."

"I guess he changed his mind since he walked out of the place a few days ago."

Rey added a packet of low-calorie sweetener to her tea and gave it a stir. "The family's not talking about his abrupt departure but I hear the father's security team is scouring the countryside for him. You think he's your intruder?"

Sasha nodded. "I do. I think he left the note and that he was the one staying in that old shack when my parents were murdered."

"Wow." Rey's eyes rounded. "That could potentially mean he witnessed what happened that night. It's possible that's what sent him over the edge. The timing is about right."

"Someone knows what happened. Leandra Brennan, Devlin Packard—someone knows." Sasha sighed. "I just have to persuade one of them to talk."

Rey studied her a moment. "How's it going with Branch? I've wanted to ask but…"

Sasha's grandmother and Rey were the only ones who knew who Brianne's father was. Both had sworn never to tell, though her grandmother had warned on numerous occasions that she felt Sasha was making a mistake.

Her grandmother had been a smart lady. Sasha *had* made a mistake.

"It's going well. He's a great guy and…" She shrugged. "I see every day that I'm here how I misjudged him. I should have listened to my grandmother."

"And me," Rey reminded her. "I always believed Branch would have jumped in with both feet to help with his child."

Sasha shook her head. "I was just so young and I had so many plans. I didn't want to throw away my dreams for married life. I was on fire to make my mark."

"No one said you had to get married." Rey smiled. "Anyway, you certainly made your mark, my friend."

Sasha laughed, the sound weary. "I definitely have." She shook her head. "But you know how it was back then. Branch would have expected us to raise her together. His family would have expected the same, plus a marriage. Certainly my grandmother would have. I can see my shortsightedness now, but at the time I could only see the future I had planned and it wasn't here, Rey. You know that. We both wanted out of this town—the sooner the better."

Rey sank back into the booth. "You're right. After what happened between me and Colt, I couldn't imagine ever coming back, much less ending up with him again under any circumstances."

Sasha felt her lips curl into a real smile. "It's amazing is what it is. You two are great together. I'm glad you came back and ended up a couple again."

"The same could happen for you," Rey suggested.

"I'm afraid my situation is a bit more complicated with a daughter who already believes she owns the world. I can't bring myself to pull the rug from under her." Sasha shook her head. "I can't bear the idea of her hating me for the decision I made."

Rey reached across the table and squeezed Sasha's hand. "You'll know what to do when the time comes."

"Hope so."

Her forearms braced on the table, Rey leaned forward. "As for this investigation, when we figure out what your mom and dad had on Packard, we're going to take him down. I, for one, can't wait. He's always been an arrogant son of a gun."

"What if it's not him?"

"Then it'll be someone like him," Rey argued. "There are some people in this world to whom human life means nothing. To kill someone standing in the way of their ultimate goal is like swatting a fly. Whoever did this, we're going to ensure he pays."

"Branch said he planned to visit my mother's office—her former office—and dig around. Find out who was doing what that year."

"Branch is a smart man," Rey said. "I'm doing a little digging in that area myself. Between the two of us, if there was something going on, we'll find it."

"There were a lot of big projects during that time frame. The stadium, the hospital."

"That decade changed the face of this city," Rey

agreed. "At least one of them created a lethal ripple. We just have to figure out which one."

She made it sound so easy.

Sasha checked the time. "I should go. I'm staking out Farr's office. I intend to catch him today. If he doesn't show I'm going to his home."

Rey grinned. "Let me know if you decide to go to the man's house. I've always wanted to see inside that lake mansion of his."

"You're on," Sasha assured her.

They paid their checks and parted ways on the sidewalk. Rey walked back to the newspaper office and Sasha climbed into her rental and headed for Farr's office. It was near the hospital, only a few short miles away from where she was. She made the necessary turns around the downtown square and then drove past the towering Packard building. The hospital was only a couple of miles beyond that iconic structure. Though the hospital was certainly not Packard's biggest development in terms of money, it was the most prestigious. Directly across the street from the hospital stood a row of boutique medical suites, one of which Farr used as an office. Sasha parked in the lot that flanked the cleverly decorated Victorian-style buildings.

To her surprise the entry door for the one on the west end was unlocked. An alarm chimed somewhere beyond the lobby as she walked inside. The interior was elegantly decorated and well-appointed. Four chairs and two Duncan Phyfe tables, along with a magazine rack, made up the tiny lobby. Distinguished-looking artwork adorned the walls. There were two doors, one to the left marked Restroom and one at the rear marked Dr. Bruce Farr. Evidently he did not have a receptionist or secretary. Sasha crossed the room and had just raised her hand to knock on the door carrying his name when it opened.

Dr. Bruce Farr blinked behind the thick lenses of his eyeglasses. "May I help you?"

"Dr. Farr?" She asked the question though she knew it was him. She had done a Google search. Though tall and distinguished in stature, his hair had grayed and thinned to near nonexistence. His skin was mottled, making him look even older in person.

"Yes, I am Dr. Farr, but I'm not taking new patients. I haven't taken new patients in nearly thirty years. I would be happy to recommend others in the area."

"You're retired, I know," Sasha said. "You serve on the board at the hospital and you continue to see a handful of longtime patients but otherwise you're retired."

His brow lined in heavy ruts. "What is it you want?"

"My name is Sasha Lenoir," she said, feeling immensely proud to inform him of this fact. "I'm here to discuss the evaluation you conducted when I was nine after my parents were murdered."

For several long seconds he stared at her. During most of those Sasha was convinced he would refuse to answer. But then he said, "I remember the case."

"Good. I have questions for you, Doctor."

Once more, he stared at her for an extended time. Just when she had decided he would say he didn't have time, he gestured to his office. "Very well. Please join me in my office. I don't have an appointment for a few minutes. I'll answer what I can until then."

He turned and walked deeper into his office, leaving the door open for her to follow. Sasha instinctively glanced over her shoulder before going inside.

"Close the door, please."

She did as he asked and then crossed the room to his desk. He indicated the lone chair waiting on her side of the desk and she sat. What remained of his once dark hair was completely gray. His eyes were a matching shade of pale gray, cold and unforgiving. She had clips of memory related to him, but none that were complete. Most were nothing more than pieces. Snippets of conversation. Him asking questions. Him staring unblinkingly at her.

"What would you like to know, Ms. Lenoir?"

"You concluded that I was making up the voices I heard the night my parents were murdered. I heard those voices, Dr. Farr. According to the county coroner, I spoke of them that very night and I told the chief of police about them a few days later. I know what I heard. Why would you insist they were my imagination at play?"

He held her gaze a long moment. "You were a very frightened and traumatized little girl. You cannot trust your memories from that painful time."

It wasn't necessary to be a shrink to know someone who had in part witnessed the murder of her parents would be traumatized and frightened. "Of course I was, but my memories are very solid from that night. You were wrong, Dr. Farr."

"You are entitled to your opinion, Ms. Lenoir, but my professional opinion hasn't changed. If you've come here to try to change my mind, I'm afraid you've wasted your time."

"Actually, it's irrelevant to me whether I change your mind, Dr. Farr. My question is, who paid you to conclude I was lying? I know it was someone with a large personal stake in the matter of whether or not my story held up in court. Perhaps Jarvis Packard or Seth Keegan. Maybe Hadden Roark."

For a moment he looked stunned, as if he couldn't believe she had voiced her accusations by listing names, or perhaps because she had hit the nail on the head, so to speak.

"You're grasping at straws, Sasha. May I call you Sasha?"

Now he was just patronizing her. "No, you may not." She laughed. "As for my grasping at straws, perhaps when my search for the truth began, that was true. Not anymore. Now I have proof."

The tiniest hint of uncertainty flared in his eyes before he could school the reaction. Oh, yes, he knew plenty about that night, just as she suspected Leandra Brennan did.

"I'm certain if you possessed proof of what you believe, you would be sitting in the chief of police's office rather than mine."

"Actually, Chief Brannigan believes me, too," she

countered. "In fact, he has reopened the case. Additionally, Marshal Branch Holloway is looking into the case, as well. Everyone knows my parents were murdered. It's time for you to speak up while you still can. I feel confident there are options for a man in your position, Dr. Farr."

She was overstepping her bounds, she knew, but the words tumbled out.

"Maybe you're simply having trouble letting go of the past, Ms. Lenoir." Dr. Farr nodded as if privy to some knowledge she did not possess. "Your mother had a similar issue, which seems to be why she could not let go of the best friend who caused her husband to stray. Such self-destructive behavior." Farr stood. "I'm afraid that's all the time I have, Ms. Lenoir. I wish you the best of luck in your pursuit."

Scarcely restraining the fury smoldering inside her, Sasha removed a business card from her purse and placed it on the man's desk. "Call me—or Chief Brannigan, if you prefer—when you decide you want to tell the truth, Dr. Farr."

She walked out of the office and climbed into her rental. If she had ever been more angry and frustrated, she had no recall of the event. She drove around for a few minutes, considered going to visit Leandra Brennan again. Branch had said he was following up on her, so Sasha drove on. Besides, she didn't trust herself to speak to the woman right now. Not after what Farr said.

Was it possible the arrogant man was correct? Had her father cheated with her mother's best friend? This didn't make sense and yet it explained why she would keep her ongoing friendship with Brennan away from her family life. This was the reason Sasha didn't recall any outings with Brennan.

"What were you thinking, Mom?"

The idea that she'd forgotten to demand a copy of Farr's report barged to the front and center of her thoughts. Anger roared inside her again. Probably he would insist all records that old had been archived or destroyed. What difference did it make? Whatever he'd said in the report was lies anyway.

She circled the cemetery and then drove to her grandmother's house. She'd fully intended to drive on past but a car parked in the driveway had her turning in. She parked beside the vehicle and rested her attention on the older man standing at the front door of the house. He looked back at her, obviously startled.

Though she had promised Branch she wouldn't come here or go anywhere else she might get trapped alone…she wasn't alone. There was a man standing on the porch. Sasha opened the door and climbed out.

"May I help you?" Since she didn't recognize the man, he likely didn't recognize her.

"Sasha?"

So maybe he did recognize her. "Are you lost?" She closed the car door and started up the walk, taking her time.

He shook his head as she approached, whether in answer to her question or in hopes of making her stop, she couldn't be sure.

"You won't remember me." He adjusted his eyeglasses. "My name is Alfred Nelson. My friends and coworkers called me—"

"Al." Sasha remembered her mother referring to Al. They worked together in the city planning office.

He nodded. "We need to talk, Sasha."

"All right." He looked harmless enough. He was old and frail, his body stooped. There was no telltale bulge in the pockets of his khaki trousers, and that was about the only place he could possibly be concealing a weapon. "Let me unlock the door and we'll go inside."

She reached into her purse and fished for the key. The house was no longer a crime scene, so they could go inside. She unlocked and pushed the door inward, then invited the older man to follow her inside. The house was cool and dark. She flipped on lights as she went. She turned to offer coffee but he had hesitated in the entry hall. He stared at the framed photograph of Sasha with her parents. It was the last one done with her parents before their murder.

"You have to stop digging into the past." His gaze shifted from the photo to her. His look was not menacing. More tired and resigned than anything.

"Why would I do that, Al?" She moved slowly toward where he stood. "I want to know the truth. Do you know what really happened that night?"

"What you're doing…" He stared at the photo again. "What you're doing is dangerous and she would not want you to be in danger. She would have done anything to protect you."

"Who killed my parents, Al?" She stood toe to toe with him now, her gaze insistent on his. He knew something—maybe everything—and she needed to hear the whole truth.

"I tried to convince her to let it go, but she refused." His gaze settled on the photograph once more.

Sasha frowned. Had this man been more than a coworker to her mother? "Were you in love with my mother, Al?"

His gaze clashed with hers, his eyes growing wide behind his glasses. "I loved her, yes, but not like you think. She was like a daughter to me." A smile touched his lips. "She was so young when she first came to the office but she had big plans. She worked harder than anyone else, so no one was surprised when she received promotion after promotion."

"Did you know about her friendship with Leandra Brennan?"

"They were like sisters growing up." He shook his head. "But Lenny took advantage of their friendship. She wanted what your mother had but her marriage was a mess. Their friendship was not a healthy relationship for Alexandra. I warned her about that, too."

"But she wouldn't listen because she loved my father," Sasha guessed. "She loved Lenny, too, so she tried to keep their relationship on some level."

"Lenny was like the snake," the man said. "The snake was cold and hungry and begged for help. Pity and kindness for his plight allowed a young girl to turn a blind eye to the fact that he was a snake. When he bit her, he reminded her that she had known what he was when she picked him up."

"Lenny was the snake," Sasha suggested.

Al nodded.

"Why were my parents murdered?" she asked, unable to breathe for fear he would stop talking.

"Because the snake was too smart. I've said too much."

He turned toward the door. Sasha couldn't allow him to leave without explaining what he meant.

"Wait." She put a hand on his arm. "You say you loved my mother like a daughter. If that's true, then why won't you help me? All I want is the truth."

He stared at Sasha, his eyes filled with regret. "The truth won't change anything."

He reached for the door again. "Don't my parents deserve justice? The truth can give me that if nothing else."

"It's too late. The truth might eventually allow for justice but it won't give you peace, Sasha. It will only bring you pain. There are some evils that are too big to stop."

Sasha followed him out the door. When he had driven away she locked up and climbed back into her rental and drove. She drove until she reached the hospital and then she pulled over and stared at the sprawling compound.

This was the biggest project her mother had been working on. This was a Packard project. Devlin—the man who had most likely left her that message and sneaked in on her twice—was a Packard. And

Leandra Brennan—aka the snake—worked for Packard.

It had to be Packard.

He had her mother and father murdered to stop them from exposing something he wanted to hide.

All Sasha had to do was find that something.

Chapter Fifteen

Sasha turned into Branch's driveway right behind him. She had driven around for an hour. Unable to bear the uncertainty, she had gone to Branch's grandmother and asked her about the rumors. Afterward, Sasha had driven around some more before she'd finally stopped and sent Branch a text. He'd called and sent her a couple of texts by then but she hadn't been ready to talk.

She wasn't sure she could now.

Everything felt wrong. She had been so certain the truth would help her to put the past behind her once and for all but that wasn't happening. The more she dug, the more questions and uncertainties she uncovered. Her parents' lives now felt skewed and off-kilter. Where was the happy childhood she had dreamed was real all these years?

Was this why her grandmother had refused to go down this path?

Had she known that hurt and disillusionment were all that waited for Sasha at the end of this journey?

She should have come to Winchester, buried her

grandmother, closed up both houses and then walked away without ever looking back.

Branch climbed out of his truck and turned in her direction. A smile spread across his handsome face.

Weakness claimed her and she barely held back the tears. How in the world was she supposed to make any of this right? She had built a career spinning other people's mistakes and she had no idea how to turn her own life around...how to tell her own truth.

How could she be disappointed in the skewed truth of her parents' lives when her own truth was way off-balance?

Did anyone get it all right? Of course not. No life was flawless. There were ups and downs and turnarounds in every life.

It was what you did with those deviations and bumps in the road that mattered.

Sasha climbed out of the rental car and walked straight up to him. "I'm not sure I can handle the truth anymore."

He pulled her into his arms and hugged her. Sasha closed her eyes and lost herself in the scent and feel of the man. He ushered her inside and closed the world out.

"You need a drink." He guided her to the sofa and left her there.

Her entire being felt bereft at the loss of contact with his. He was wrong. She didn't need a drink. She needed his body wrapped around hers so thoroughly that it was impossible to tell where one of them began and the other one ended. She wanted to lose herself in him in that way. She didn't want to think. She only wanted to feel.

He thrust a small glass of amber liquid in front of her. "Drink it. You'll feel better."

She didn't believe him but she drank it anyway. Scotch. She shuddered with the burn of it sliding down her throat. "Thank you."

Branch sat down in the chair across the coffee table from her and knocked back his own shot of Scotch. He placed his glass on the table and then settled his hat next to it. He ran his fingers through his hair and set his attention fully on her. "Tell me what happened."

"The reason I don't remember my mother's best friend is because they never saw each other outside the occasional lunch. Leandra Brennan—Lenny—and my mother grew up together. They went to college together, got married the same summer. They were best friends—like sisters. Until something happened between my father and her. According to Arlene—"

"You talked to her today?"

Sasha nodded. "She said my grandmother never wanted me to know any of this, so they kept my mother's secret. There was a big barbecue when my mother was pregnant with me. Lenny and her husband were fighting and everyone was drinking except my mother. Anyway, at some point that evening my mother caught Lenny and my dad kissing. Arlene said Mother would never elaborate if there was something more going on than just two drunk people doing something stupid. But she and Lenny stopped being friends for a long while. Apparently they had only recently started having the occasional lunch together right before my parents died."

Branch shook his head. "It's easy to forget that our parents are mere humans, too, and they've made mistakes."

Sasha stared at the empty glass in her hands. "I was a child when they died. My every memory is of these perfect people who were above mere human mistakes. I don't even remember ever being scolded. All the memories other than the night they were killed are sweet and cherished and perfect."

"Just because you discovered a painful truth doesn't mean all the happy truths are no longer real or relevant."

She placed her glass on the table and wrung her hands. "I found Dr. Farr. He refuses, of course, to change his opinion of my story. He, apparently, was aware of my father's infidelity, which makes me wonder if it was such common knowledge why I hadn't heard of it before."

"Maybe it came out in the investigation but wasn't necessarily common knowledge."

"Maybe."

"Or," Branch offered, "maybe your grandmother suggested that Luther look into Alexandra's former best friend because of what had happened."

Sasha nodded. "You're probably right. G'ma would likely have considered the possibility. I know I certainly would have." She looked to Branch. "Did you talk to Brennan today?"

"I did." Branch stared at the floor a moment. "She came up with an even crazier story. In fact, she broke down into tears and blubbered her way through most of it. She explained how she and your father had been having an affair and your mother found out and intended to divorce him and take everything. She thinks your father intended to have her killed and things went terribly wrong."

"Are you serious? She said those things?"

He met Sasha's gaze. "She did. She claims she was trying to put her marriage back together but that he wouldn't leave her alone. She and your mother were having secret lunches to discuss how to handle the situation."

Sasha shook her head. "I don't believe it. I would remember that kind of tension."

"At one point you did say they were arguing more during those final weeks."

She had said that. "It was about work. I remember distinctly that he thought she was working too much and she complained that he needed to find a new job."

This—all of this—grew more confusing by the moment.

"Wait." She had almost forgotten to tell him about Alfred Nelson. "I spoke to Mr. Nelson, the man who worked in the office with my mother. He was knocking on the door of my grandmother's house when I drove past, so I stopped and talked to him. He urged me to stop digging around in the past. He said it would only hurt me the way it did my mother. He alluded to how Brennan betrayed my mother."

"At least it sounds like everyone has gotten their story straight."

He was right. Farr, Brennan and Nelson were all suddenly spouting basically the same story. "Seems rather convenient."

Branch nodded. "It does. I think maybe we need to take today's influx of information with a grain of salt."

"Nelson also said something like there are some evils too big to stop. Do you think he was referring to Jarvis Packard?"

"Packard would certainly fit the description."

Sasha shot to her feet. She couldn't sit still any longer. "This is just too much. I don't know why my grandmother didn't simply explain the situation to me once I was an adult. I shouldn't have to be doing this." She crossed the room and stared out the window.

Branch moved up behind her. Her body reacted instantly. How she would love to turn around and fall into his arms.

"You don't have to do this, Sasha. Knowing the truth—whatever it might be—won't bring your parents back. It won't make you feel any better about the fact that your grandmother didn't want to talk about it. It won't change anything unless it helps to put a killer behind bars."

"And clears my father's name," she reminded him.

"If you want to clear your father's name and find justice for your parents, then you have to do this. Otherwise, you don't have to go down this path. No one will fault you if you decide you've had enough."

He made it seem like such an easy decision.

"It's not that simple," she argued.

"It's never that simple," he agreed.

She turned around, her body so close to his she could feel the heat of his skin beneath his clothes. "Why are you helping me?"

It wasn't what she'd intended to ask when she opened her mouth but it was what came out.

He frowned down at her. "Why wouldn't I help you?"

"That's not an answer."

He searched her eyes as if the motive for her demand might show itself, but she couldn't let him see that what she wanted was to push him away. To stop this thing before it was completely out of control. While they could still look back and call what they'd shared the past few days nice, a friend helping a friend.

"I told you I've always wanted a do-over. I've wished more times than I can count for an opportunity to spend time with you again."

Sasha thought of all the lies she had discovered… all the confusing things that didn't add up. Was that the legacy she wanted to leave her daughter? A box of untruths and a trail of uncertainties.

She grabbed Branch and pulled his face down to hers. She kissed him with all the hunger and desire strumming through her. A minute from now he would never look at her the same. A minute from now he would know the one truth that mattered more than all the others.

His arms went around her and he pulled her against him, deepened the kiss, taking control, and she wept with the knowledge that this would be the only time.

When she could bear the sweet tenderness no longer, she pushed him away. When he released her, his eyes glazed with need, she crossed the room, found her bag and pulled out her cell phone.

"What's going on, Sasha?" He watched her, worry in his eyes now. He understood something was very, very wrong.

Something besides her murdered parents and their secrets. Besides her dead grandmother and the truths she chose to take with her to her grave. Besides the urgent need still roaring through her body.

"I've never wanted a do-over of that night, Branch."

He stared at her, confusion clouding his face. "I don't understand."

"That night was amazing." She smiled, swiped at an errant tear that escaped her iron hold. "It was the night I had waited for since I was thirteen years old and first fell madly in love with you."

He smiled, his own eyes suspiciously bright. "I remember thinking that if you would have me I would be the happiest guy in the world, but I always thought you had other plans."

His confession hurt more than she wanted to

admit. How could they not have known? Had they been too busy running away from their lives here that they couldn't see each other clearly?

"I did and that was my mistake. I couldn't stop running toward the future long enough to see what was right here in my present. I had all these big plans. I was going to make my mark, make a name for myself. I was never again going to be the orphaned girl who lost her whole world. I was going to be someone who mattered."

"First—" he took a step in her direction "—you were always someone who mattered. To your grandmother. To my family. To *me*."

More of those damned tears flowed down her cheeks. "But I couldn't see that. I allowed the need to prove myself to rule my life and I made a terrible, terrible mistake. One I'm certain you won't be able to forgive me for."

He reached up and tugged a wisp of hair from her damp cheek. "I'm fairly certain you have nothing to worry about on that score. Whatever you did or didn't do when you left, you don't owe me an explanation. I'm here for you now and I'll be here for you tomorrow. I want to be a part of your life—a part of your daughter's life."

Sasha stared at him, her entire being aching. Her fingers tightened around the phone full of pictures of her precious daughter. "She's *your* daughter, too."

The kaleidoscope of evolving emotions on his face took her breath. He went from shock to amazement and then to anger.

"What do you mean?"

"I mean, the one time we were together Brianne was conceived. I didn't know until weeks later and…"

And what?

She made the decision not to tell him. She chose to go on with her life and to not look back.

"Why didn't you call me?"

His voice was hollow. That, too, would change in a moment. "My grandmother said you had accepted a big promotion in Chicago. I had that job offer in New York. The timing was just wrong."

"Timing?"

Now the fire was in his tone. He was angry. She didn't blame him. She deserved whatever he decided to throw her way.

"I should have told you." She took a breath. "I promised myself I would a thousand times, but it never felt like the right time, so I never did."

The entire scene had taken on a dreamlike quality. Sasha felt uncertain of herself and at the same time completely at peace with the decision she had made.

She had told him. At long last. Regardless of what happened next, she had done the right thing.

He looked away, shook his head. "I need some air and to think."

She nodded. "I understand."

He walked out of the room. Moments later she heard the back door close.

She tapped her contacts list and put through a call to Rey. "I need to talk to you."

Five minutes later Sasha had left a note for Branch,

telling him that she would spend the night with Rey, and then she left to give him the space he needed to come to terms with her announcement. Her soul ached as if she were driving away from that night all those years ago all over again.

She and Branch had made love and then they'd walked away from each other without ever looking back.

They had both made a mistake, but hers was the far more egregious one.

REY MET HER at the Lenoir house.

As much as Sasha would love to lose herself to a bottle of wine, a buzz would not help. She needed to keep her mind busy—to focus on something until she could bear to properly consider what she had done.

Branch knew he had a daughter now.

Now she had to tell Brianne. Maybe it would be better to bring her here and to do the introductions in person.

"What's the plan?" Rey glanced around the dusty old house. "I've got pizza and wine ordered. We have about half an hour before it arrives."

"Pizza and wine?" Since when did the two pizza places in Winchester deliver wine?

"Brian is bringing us dinner. Don't worry—he's not staying. He and his love have plans. He's just dropping off the food and a few other things we might need."

Brian Peterson worked with Rey at the newspaper. He and Rey had been best friends in school and later it had been the three of them. As close as Sasha and Rey always were, there had been a special bond between Rey and Brian.

"I'm afraid to ask what kinds of things."

Rey shrugged. "Nightshirts, sleeping bags, toothbrushes. Just a few necessities."

Sasha was really grateful for good friends like Rey and Brian.

She instantly chastised herself for leaving Branch out. He was a good friend, too. She hoped they would be able to be friends again.

"So." Rey turned to her. "What's the plan?"

Sasha started to say that she had no plan, but then she realized she had a very important plan. "I want to take this place apart."

Rey made a face. "Define *take apart*."

"I want to look inside and under everything. If it's here, I want to find it."

Another of those strange expressions twisted Rey's face. *"It?"*

Sasha nodded. "I have no idea what it is, but we're going to look until we find it—unless you have objections."

Rey shook her head. "None. Except maybe I'll text Brian and add gloves to the needs list."

"Good idea." Sasha smiled. She didn't have to see it to know it was sad; it felt sad. She felt sad. But this was the first step toward moving forward. She did not want to leave this painful black cloud hanging over her daughter's life.

Her daughter deserved happiness.

Her daughter deserved to know her father.

Branch deserved to know his daughter.

And Sasha intended to have the truth—whatever it turned out to be—and justice for her parents.

Chapter Sixteen

Branch knocked on the door of his grandmother's home and waited for her to answer. He usually called before showing up just to make sure she was home, but this time he couldn't bring himself to make the call. He needed to see her in person. He needed to see her face when she answered his question.

Eighty-five-year-old Arlene Holloway opened the door. Branch reminded himself of her age and her station in his family. He reached for calm. Upsetting this woman was the last thing he wanted to do and in his current state he didn't completely trust himself to make good decisions.

"Branch, is something wrong?"

He hadn't called and he always did. "Yes, ma'am. I'm a little upset. May I come in?"

"Well, of course." She drew the door open wide and shuffled back out of his way. "Is Sasha all right? Where is she?"

The sweet little old lady craned her neck to see through the darkness beyond the door.

"She's with Rey Anderson."

Arlene nodded. "Rey's doing a fine job with the newspaper. Far better than her uncle Phillip ever did. He was too busy chasing the widows around town."

Branch smiled in spite of the circumstances. His grandmother always knew how to put a smile on his face, even when she wasn't trying. "I hear he went down to Florida for spring break."

"Spring break?" she grumbled as she locked the door. "He looks like a spring break. The man needs to find a hobby that doesn't involve chasing skirts."

Branch knew better than to encourage her. "I have some questions I need to ask you, Gran."

She stared at him from behind the thick lenses of her glasses. She blinked. "Do we need a stiff drink to make them go down easier?"

"Possibly." No point pretending.

"Have a seat over there." She gestured toward the living room. "I'll round up Walker's bourbon."

His grandfather had been dead for ten years and his grandmother still called the stash of bourbon she kept his. Branch knew for a fact she'd purchased a new fifth of bourbon at least twice in those ten years. Most of the time she had Branch's father pick it up. It wouldn't be proper for her to be seen in the liquor store, much less buying something. She shuffled over to the sofa, two sipping glasses and the fifth of bourbon clasped in her gnarled hands. She poured, passed a glass to him and lifted the other to her lips.

When they'd downed a swallow, she looked him square in the eye and asked, "What happened?"

"Did you know Sasha's daughter was my child?"

Since Sasha left, she had sent him a dozen photos of Brianne via text, some going back to when the girl was a baby in diapers. The younger photos were like looking at candid shots of himself as a kid.

Every time he looked at the photos he felt a punch to his gut. How the hell had this happened? Why would Sasha have kept a secret like this from him? For a dozen years no less.

He should have gone after her.

"I had my suspicions," Arlene confessed. "But I never knew for sure. Vi never said a word—I imagine because Sasha told her not to. It was like what happened to Sasha's parents. We never discussed it. I tried once and she said no and that was that. We respected each other that way, son. When you get older you realize how important that one thing is. When your loved ones vanish one by one and your health goes by the wayside, you still got your self-respect and the respect of your good friends—if you're lucky."

Branch shook his head. "Part of me wants to raise hell. She kept this child from me for twelve long years."

"Would that fix anything?" she asked. "Make you feel any better?"

He downed his bourbon, winced at the burn. "Not likely on either count."

"Well, there's your answer. If I had my guess, she kept this information from the girl, too. She's going to have herself enough trouble explaining that decision. She won't need any trouble from you on top of that. I think a little patience is in order. And maybe some understanding. She was young and terrified. She's already done all the hard work. Now all you have to do is enjoy. She's a beautiful girl and, from all the things Vi told me about her, smart as a whip to boot."

Branch nodded. "We'll figure this out."

Arlene smiled. "I think you already did."

"I think you're right."

He had a daughter. A beautiful daughter who was smart and who deserved the best dad he could be.

"I guess I should call the folks."

"You might want to have another sip of that bourbon first. Your mama has been pining for a grandchild for years. She will be over the moon."

His cell vibrated and he slid it from his pocket in case it was Sasha. He checked the screen and frowned. Not Sasha. "Hey, Billy, what's going on?"

It was a little late in the evening for the chief of police to be making social calls. Branch braced for trouble. He'd had a text from Sasha not an hour ago, so hopefully all was well with her.

"Hey, Branch, I've got a situation you need to have a look at."

Oh, hell. "What's the location?"

"Alfred Nelson's place. Looks like a suicide but there's a strange note."

"On my way."

When he stood and tucked his phone away, his grandmother frowned up at him. "You have to go?"

"Yes, ma'am. Thank you for the advice and the

drink." Though it was a good thing he hadn't taken more than a sip.

"Not to worry, son. I'll finish it off for you." She shot him a wink.

Branch gave her a hug, her body so frail beneath his big arms. "Love you, Gran."

"Love you. Now you be nice to Sasha. She's had enough troubles in her life. She deserves good things and she's just given you a miraculous gift. Enjoy it. Don't fret over how long it took her to get around to giving it."

"Yes, ma'am."

On the porch, he settled his hat into place and headed for his truck. His grandmother was a very smart lady.

ALFRED NELSON LIVED ALONE. His wife had died four years ago. According to Burt Johnston, who knew everyone in the county, Al, as his friends called him, had been instrumental in Alexandra Lenoir being hired in the planning and zoning office. He'd also gone to bat for her big promotion two years later. Though he had worked in that office for a half a dozen years before she came along, he had not possessed the degree he felt the supervisory position deserved. He had insisted that Alexandra was the right person for the job.

It appeared that at some point after lunch today he had decided to end his life. He'd tied a length of clothesline around the ceiling fan and made a noose. Then he'd climbed back up the ladder, put the noose around his neck and stepped off the rung. The ladder had been knocked onto its side by his swaying body.

But before he'd done all that, he'd written a note to Sasha, explaining that her parents' deaths were his fault. He hadn't really meant for everything to turn out the way it had, but he'd made a terrible, terrible mistake. He'd gone to their house with the intention of killing Brandon Lenoir and taking Alexandra far away to be his. He had wanted to have her all to himself for a very long time. But things had gone wrong and a struggle over the gun had taken Alexandra's life. He'd then killed Brandon Lenoir and attempted to make it look like a murder-suicide. His voice was the one Sasha had heard that night. It was all him.

"What do you make of his confession?" Billy asked, his tone heavy with skepticism.

"About the same thing you do, I suspect." Branch shook his head. "This would mean that Alfred was the intruder, and we both know he was in no physical condition to be running through the woods, much less to break into anyone's home. When Sasha spoke to him today, he warned her to stop digging and that some evils were too big to stop."

The strangest part of the entire scene were the empty file drawers in his home office. Any personal or professional papers he had kept were gone.

"Someone is tying up loose ends." Billy watched as the coroner's two assistants removed the body from the scene.

That was the part that worried Branch. "I should

talk to Sasha about this before she hears some other way."

"Devlin Packard is still missing," Billy warned. "I don't know if this is his work—frankly, I don't think so—but he's part of this somehow. I've got this feeling that his disappearance and all this are not just coincidence."

Devlin was another of those pieces that simply refused to fit into a slot, like long-missing puzzle parts that were too faded and misshapen to go into place. Yet it was instinctively understood that those pieces belonged in this particular puzzle. There were apparently a whole slew of secrets among the players from twenty-seven years ago and each of those secrets fit together somehow.

"Did you talk to Leandra Brennan again?" Branch wondered if Billy had gotten the same story he did.

"As a matter of fact, she was very forthcoming about her relationship with Sasha's mother and her father. Brennan thinks that during the time she had the affair with Brandon that Alexandra was involved with Alfred." Billy hitched his head toward the body bag. "Perfect timing for her to offer up that previously withheld information. Funny how that keeps happening."

Branch shook his head. "Give me a call if you learn anything new."

Billy gave him a nod. "Will do."

From the Nelson residence, Branch drove to the Lenoir house. Sasha had told him that she and Rey were spending the night there. He wasn't happy about the idea but at least she wasn't alone.

The porch light was on as he climbed out of his truck. He walked past Rey's car. Sasha had left her rental at Rey's. The backyard was completely dark. He wasn't happy about the idea that someone could get all the way to the house from the woods without being seen. For insurance purposes Viola had kept the power and water turned on to the old house, but she hadn't exactly ensured the maintenance was taken care of. Sasha needed to bear that in mind.

He knocked on the door. Half a minute later it opened and Rey beamed a smile at him.

"Branch." She opened the door wide. "Come on in."

He followed her inside and Sasha appeared at the bottom of the stairs. "Hey."

He gave her a nod.

"I'll get back to work." Rey flashed Sasha a smile before bounding up the stairs.

"Is everything okay?" Sasha asked, her expression as uncertain as he felt.

"Billy called. Alfred Nelson is dead."

"What happened?"

"He appears to have committed suicide. He left a note addressed to you."

He repeated the contents of the note and she immediately started to shake her head.

"He insisted that he thought of my mother as a daughter," she argued. "He helped her get the job, pushed for her promotion—both of which sound more like what someone would do for a daughter. I didn't get the impression that he was lying to me or that his feelings were anything other than platonic. This doesn't make sense."

"None at all. And, by the way, in her statement this afternoon to Billy, Leandra Brennan just happened to recall a possible affair between Nelson and your mother."

"We're too close." Sasha's gaze locked with his. "They're worried, so they're attempting to cover all the bases. They hadn't counted on me remembering anything from that night. They thought they'd shut me down."

"They still could."

She looked away. "I'm being careful. Rey is here with me."

"Promise me you won't take any chances, Sasha. I don't like that you're here instead of at my place."

"I'm grateful you feel that way, Branch. I honestly didn't know what to expect after you learned the secret I've kept all these years."

"The decision you made was as much my fault as it was yours," he said. As much as he wanted to be angry, that was the truth of the matter. "If I had behaved differently, you might have felt more inclined to be forthcoming. Either way, what's done is done. We should go from here, not dwell in the past."

She hugged him and for a moment he couldn't move. Maybe it was the shock of her sudden display of affection. Finally, he hugged her back. Whatever else they were, they were friends. They had a daughter. There were a lot of things that needed to be worked out, but this didn't have to be one of those things.

When she drew back she crossed her arms over her chest in a protective manner. "We're going through everything in the house. If there's anything else to find, we plan on finding it tonight."

"Keep the doors locked and stay on alert. Billy thinks someone is tying up loose ends."

The idea made way too much sense and Branch did not like it one little bit.

She nodded. "We will."

"Call me if you need anything. I'm only eight or nine minutes away."

"I'll call if we need anything. I promise."

As much as he had hoped she would ask him to stay, she didn't. She needed space and time. He understood that. Still, this was not the best time to want distance.

But Rey was here.

That was the only reason he was able to climb into his truck and drive away.

Even then he didn't feel particularly good about it.

Nine minutes later he was in his own house and ready to call it a night, though he doubted he would sleep a wink.

Notification that he had received a text message had him reaching for his cell. The message was from an unknown number. A New York area code. Not Sasha. Her name and number were in his contact list.

He opened the message and read the words.

So, I hear you're my dad.

His heart surged into his throat.
Sasha had told her.
He hadn't anticipated that happening so fast.

Yes. I apologize for the delay in being around. As long as you let me, I plan to make up for it.

Holding his breath, he hit Send.
He didn't breathe again until another text message appeared.

I can handle that.

He smiled and typed a quick response.

Great.

Then he called his parents.
His mother answered on the second ring. "Is everything all right, Branch?"
"Everything's fine," he assured her. "I know it's late, but this couldn't wait."

Chapter Seventeen

Thursday, March 28

It was barely daylight when Sasha awakened the next morning. She and Rey had stayed up far too late going through drawers and boxes and closets. She'd spent a lot of that time talking to Brianne. She'd at first thought she would wait until she was back home to talk to her in person, but considering her grandmother had just died and the rest of what was going on, Sasha had decided a live video chat was the perfect compromise.

Brianne had taken the news in stride. She'd been waiting a long time to learn the identity of her father. Sasha was grateful for her patience and her understanding. One of her first requests was for his cell phone number. Branch had let Sasha know that Brianne had contacted him.

Sasha was particularly thankful that Branch was handling the news so well. For years she had worried about how this would all go down. She should have known her daughter would handle the situation well. Brianne was a very well-adjusted and confident young girl. Sasha was very proud of her.

Branch was a lucky guy to get a daughter as awesome as Brianne.

Sasha ventured into the kitchen. Rey had brought wine and bottled water but she hadn't thought of coffee. Sasha needed coffee badly. She could probably run into town and grab coffee and muffins or something before Rey was up The woman had been like a mini tornado last night. They'd gone through nearly everything in the house. There was nothing else here—nothing that helped with the case, anyway.

So much had happened the past couple of days. There was no question now about whether her parents were murdered or not. They were. Several suspects had come to their attention. Leandra Brennan, Alfred Nelson, Jarvis Packard, Seth Keegan and Hadden Roark. Then there was Devlin Packard. But Sasha had him pegged as a witness rather than a killer.

She grabbed her purse, the keys and her phone and eased out the front door. Locking it behind her, she dropped her phone into her bag.

"You should have listened to me."

Sasha whipped around to face the voice.

She recognized the face from her Google search. Devlin Packard stared at her, his eyes wide with fear or uncertainty—perhaps insanity.

Her first thought was to scream. She resisted the impulse.

"Devlin." She reminded herself to breathe. "I'm

glad you came back. I've been trying to find answers. I could use your help."

He stared at her, his expression trapped somewhere between fear and distrust.

"Would you like to come inside? I was going for breakfast. I can bring you back something to eat."

She prayed he was hungry.

He grabbed her by the arm. "You have to come with me now."

Her bag and keys hit the floor.

Fear surged into her throat. Now would be the time to scream. But if she did, any trust she had built with this man would vanish.

Could she trust him not to kill her?

She reminded herself he'd had opportunities before and he hadn't killed her.

He moved faster and faster across the backyard. Dew on the knee-deep grass dampened her jeans. She stumbled in an effort to keep up with his long strides. They hit the tree line and she realized where they were going. The rising sun was abruptly blocked from view by the dark woods.

"You were living in the shack when my parents died."

He yanked her closer as if he feared she might try to take off.

Sasha allowed him to draw her nearer and she didn't fight him. He needed to sense that she trusted him. If he had seen something—if he knew anything about what happened that night—she needed him cooperative.

Her heart was pounding hard by the time they reached the shack. He pushed her through the door and followed her inside, leaving the door standing open, perhaps for the meager light. Still, the interior remained in near-total darkness. She wished she had her phone for the flashlight app.

"You shouldn't have come back asking questions. Big mistake. Big mistake." He was agitated, shifting from foot to foot, shaking his head.

She wrapped her arms around herself and tried to remember what she had seen inside this shack. An old quilt. Some trash.

"I just wanted to know what happened to my mom and dad." She said this softly, quietly, like the child she was when her parents died. Strange, no matter how many years had passed, she still felt like a hurt and lonely child when she allowed herself to be transported back to that time.

"They'll kill you just like they killed them." He leaned close to her. She fought the urge to shudder. "That's why I came back."

"Thank you." *Keep him talking.* Rey would wake up and realize she was gone. She would call Branch.

"I found out you were back and digging around. You should have just buried your grandma and gone back to the big city. You shouldn't have started asking questions. I knew they'd find out and do to you what they did to them."

"Who?" she asked. "Who hurt my parents?"

He shook his head again, moved toward the door,

stared outside as if he feared someone might have followed them. "They're dead. Can't bring them back."

Was he talking about her parents?

"We should call the police and tell them what really happened," she urged. The more agitated he grew, the more nervous she felt. But he knew something. She was certain.

He swung around and glared at her. "Are you crazy? The police can't stop them. No one can."

Fear swelled inside her. "You're right. I don't know what I was thinking."

For a few seconds it was so quiet she could hear him breathing, could hear the blood sweeping through her veins.

"Your mother let me stay here because she felt sorry for me. She was nice to me."

"Were you in trouble?"

He glared at her. "I was always in trouble. I couldn't do anything right."

"So my mother was helping you." Sasha mustered up a smile. "She liked helping people."

He shook his head again, so hard it couldn't have been comfortable. "She shouldn't have helped me."

"Do you think they hurt her and my dad because she helped you?" If her heart pounded any faster it would surely burst from her chest.

"They think I don't know but I do." He looked outside again. "They're coming for me. I'm too tired to hide from them anymore. I can't keep running."

Sasha looked outside. "Who's coming?"

"I have to show you before they come. I might not get another chance."

Sasha didn't see or hear anyone. But if he had something to show her it could be important. "Okay."

He went to the farthest corner of the shack and pawed around on the floor.

She had the perfect opportunity to run. His back was to her. She was standing next to the door. He was several feet away. But she needed to stay…to see what he intended to show her.

He stood, turned around and moved toward her. "I kept this. They don't know about it. I wanted you to have it."

He handed her a wad of papers. "If they find them, they'll take them and then you'll never have what you need."

"I'll keep them safe," she promised. Her hands shook as her fingers wrapped around the pages.

The distant sound of a voice jerked their attention to the door.

"They're coming," he murmured.

He shoved the door closed and turned to her. "Stay away from the door. They're here to kill us."

BRANCH WAS JUST about to walk out the door when his cell vibrated with an incoming call. He didn't recognize the number but it was local. "Holloway."

"Branch, this is Rey. Sasha is missing. Her purse and keys were lying on the porch but I can't find her. There are some guys here—they look like SWAT or something. They want to search the property."

Branch was already climbing into his truck. "Do not allow them to search the property. Call Colt and Billy. I'm on my way."

Branch had a feeling the SWAT types Rey meant were some of Packard's security force, and they had no jurisdiction beyond the Packard facility and certainly not on private property. Unfortunately he doubted a little technicality like that had ever stopped them.

It took him six minutes to drive to the Lenoir house, and Franklin County Sheriff Colton "Colt" Tanner's truck was already there.

Rey was on the porch.

"They're in the backyard!" she shouted, pointing around the corner of the house.

As Branch rushed around the corner of the house Billy's truck roared into the driveway. Branch didn't slow down. Rey would send him in the right direction.

Colt had stopped the four-man team dressed in black and armed to the gills at the tree line where the backyard faded into the dark woods.

All four men in black seemed to track Branch's movements as he approached.

"US Marshal Branch Holloway," he called out, identifying himself. "Chief of Police Brannigan is here, as well. You gentlemen are trespassing."

"Morning, Branch." Colt nodded. "I was just explaining to these fine gentlemen that this is private property."

"We have reason to believe our employer's mentally unstable son is in those woods. He may present a danger to himself and to others. We have orders to take him back to the hospital."

If he was here, Branch knew where he had gone. "Sheriff, if you and the chief will babysit these gentlemen, I'll have a look around."

Colt gave him a nod and Branch walked into the forest. He barely restrained the need to run until he was out of sight of the security team. Then he ran like hell. When he spotted the shack, he slowed down, stayed in the cover of the dense foliage.

Quietly and straining to hear any sound, he moved closer.

He couldn't be sure if the man was armed or not. Rather than risk going in, he called out. "Sasha, it's me. You in there?"

"Branch!"

Shuffling and muffled sounds told him that Devlin was with her. He held himself back when he wanted to rush inside and rescue her. He couldn't do anything that might get her hurt…or worse.

"He's my friend," Sasha said.

Branch eased closer.

"I can't protect you," a male voice growled.

Branch wrenched the door open. "I can protect her." He looked from the man who whirled to face him and then to Sasha. She looked unharmed but shaken. "I can protect you both," he said to the man he recognized as Devlin Packard.

Packard shook his head. "They'll kill us if they get the chance."

Branch thought of the assault rifles the men in black had been carrying.

"Stay in the shack and lie down on the floor." He looked to Sasha. "You, too."

Sasha quickly obeyed. She grabbed the man by the hand and pulled him down, too. Branch took a position in front of the door. He called Billy. "I'm at the shack and they're both here. He's terrified of the guys in black. He thinks they've been sent here to kill him and Sasha. We need to get these two out of here and back to city hall."

Thirty-five minutes were required to clear the area. Branch sweat blood every second of every minute. Knowing the kind of powerful man Packard was, he could have several four-man teams combing the woods. Branch kept expecting to be overtaken from one direction or the other.

When Billy and his officers arrived to escort them out of the woods, Branch took his first deep breath.

"The security team has been relocated to city hall via the sheriff's department."

Branch was glad to hear it. He opened the door and held his hand out for Sasha. "It's clear."

As soon as she was out of the shack she went up on tiptoe and whispered in his ear. "Don't treat him like a prisoner."

Branch nodded and offered his hand to the man still lying on the floor of the shack. "It's okay to come out now, Devlin. No one is going to hurt you."

The man took his hand and pulled himself up. He looked around as he stepped out.

"This is Chief of Police Brannigan," Branch explained. "He's going to make sure we get safely out of the woods so we can explain what happened."

Still looking uncertain, the man nodded.

ANOTHER HALF HOUR was required to get everyone transported to city hall. Devlin Packard was settled into an interview room and a court-appointed attorney was on his way. They were trying to move fast, before Jarvis Packard showed up and started to swing his weight around.

Billy, Sasha and Branch stood over the conference table and considered the drawings Devlin had given her. Several of the drawings showed a woman watching through the windows of a house. Sasha presumed it was her childhood home and that the woman was her mother. The other pictures showed men in black looking in those same windows. Sasha thought of the men in black who had shown up to take Devlin. Were these Packard's security thugs in the drawings? Why would they be looking in the windows of her childhood home?

She shook her head. "I'm not sure what any of this means."

"I think I am." Branch picked up his cell phone and tapped on the screen. Then he turned to Billy and said, "Sasha needs to see Devlin. He wouldn't talk to you, but he'll talk to her."

"I think he will," Sasha agreed. "If there's any chance he can explain what this means, it's worth a shot."

"We can try." Billy opened the door. "You and I can watch from the observation room."

"That'll work," Branch agreed.

Billy led the way to the interview room. Branch passed his cell phone and the drawings to Sasha. "Ask him if the woman in the drawings is this woman."

Sasha stared at the image on the screen: Leandra Brennan's face from twenty or so years ago. The photo was from a feature article in the local newspaper. She had noticed it when she'd done an internet search on the woman. Sasha thought of the woman's accusations and renewed fury whipped through her. Then she suddenly understood what Branch was thinking. Their gazes locked and she nodded her understanding of his instructions.

Bracing herself, Sasha entered the interview room and sat down at the table. "Do you need anything to drink or to eat, Devlin?"

He shook his head, the jerkiness of the motion warning her he was still agitated.

"I think we've figured out what you've been trying to tell us, Devlin." She placed the drawings on the table in front of him. He looked from one to the next, the pages faded with time.

"Is this the woman you were watching and drawing?" She showed him the image on the screen of Branch's cell phone.

He nodded, the movement frantic. "She's not a nice person."

"Did she hurt my parents?"

He shrugged. "She only watched. The men—" he tapped another of his drawings "—they are the ones who hurt them."

"You're sure about that?" Sasha reminded herself to breathe.

He nodded. "My father always stopped people who got in his way."

Sasha forced her trembling lips into a smile. "Thank you, Devlin. That helps a lot."

When she had reclaimed the drawings and walked out of the room, she stared at Branch. "He identified her. Why was she watching my family?"

But she knew the answer. The affair, or whatever it was that had happened between Brennan and Sasha's father.

"Two of my officers are bringing her in now," Billy assured her. "The moment Devlin identified her, I ordered a unit to pick her up."

"What about Packard?" Branch asked.

"I have my best detectives headed to his house now."

Was this really happening? Would Sasha finally know the truth?

Two hours dragged by. Sasha was keenly aware of every second.

And finally Leandra Brennan confessed. With Branch at her side, Sasha watched from the observation room via the one-way mirror.

"He loved me more than her but she wouldn't let him go. I tried to do the right thing since she was pregnant. But then I saw him again years later—after he lost his job. We ran into each other. He was drinking and I helped him get home. I knew after that day that he was still in love with me. So I decided to make it happen."

"How did you do that?" Billy asked.

"I knew Mr. Packard would never allow anyone to get in the way of his hospital plans. So I set her up. I made her believe that Packard was taking short-cuts. I gave her altered site plans. I made Mr. Packard believe she wanted money." She laughed. "For such a brilliant man he bought the story hook, line and sinker. He ordered his men to take care of her." She frowned. "Brandon wasn't supposed to be home that night. He was supposed to be with me. Only Alexandra and Sasha were supposed to die. But he got in the way and I lost him. If Sasha had died that night, no one would ever have known."

Sasha couldn't listen to any more. She left the observation room.

The idea that her mother had died because her best friend wanted her husband made Sasha sick. She would never know for certain how guilty her father was in the whole mess, if at all. But she did know that her father had tried to protect her mother in the end. That meant something.

Branch stepped into the corridor. "You hanging in there?"

Sasha shrugged then nodded. "I think so. I just need some time to think."

"Rey is waiting to take you home with her. I'm

staying here until I'm sure Packard and his minions are all accounted for and arrested."

"Thank you, Branch. I couldn't have done this without you."

He gave her a nod. "We'll talk soon."

He was right. They did need to talk. *Soon.*

Chapter Eighteen

Monday, April 1

Sasha stood in the backyard of her childhood home and stared at the woods. As a child she had loved this place. She had explored every inch of those woods. She turned back to the house. It was a shame for it to continue to fall even further into disrepair. The house could be a home for a family. She would contact a Realtor and a contractor to get started with the cleanout and renovations.

There was a lot of work but it was time to move on from the past.

She had decided to keep her grandmother's house. It felt more like home than this place, or any other, for that matter. Besides, how could she part with the home her grandmother had loved so much? She couldn't. She would pass it down to her daughter when the time came.

Though she had reached a number of decisions, there were more to make.

The breeze shifted, wrapping her in the cool morning air. She hugged her arms around herself. She had taken an extended leave of absence from her firm. Brianne would finish her school year online. Together they would spend the summer exploring their options.

Jarvis Packard had lawyered up and was denying any knowledge of the story Leandra Brennan had told. Not that Sasha had expected him to own his part in the deaths of her parents. Brennan had also insisted that Packard had ordered Alfred Nelson's death, as well. Unless Brennan had proof of her allegations, there was a very good chance Packard would walk away unscathed. Sasha was grateful to know the truth finally and she felt confident Brennan would spend a very long time in prison for her heinous deeds.

Brennan had conspired to end the life of Sasha's mother—her former best friend. Brennan had wanted Sasha's mother's life for her own. The cost had been irrelevant.

Sasha shuddered. She was extremely grateful to Devlin Packard for helping to reveal the persons responsible for the murders of her parents. She might never have known for certain without him. He was headed back to his posh resort-like rehab facility. Sasha wished him well.

More important, Branch had stood with her through this journey into the past. He was the real hero here.

The sound of a vehicle arriving drew her attention to the house. Speak of the devil. That would be Branch. She walked around front and watched as he climbed out of his truck. As he moved toward her, anticipation fizzed in her belly. She would never tire of watching him move or hearing him talk. He smiled. Or seeing him smile.

"Morning."

"Good morning." They met on the front walk. It was actually visible now. Branch had sent the lawn service that took care of his grandmother's property to tame the jungle around this house.

"Billy called," he told her. "Dr. Farr cut a deal with the district attorney. He's going to testify that Jarvis Packard gave him a position on the hospital board of directors in exchange for his expert testimony about you."

Sasha pressed her fingers to her mouth. She had known Farr was lying. When she found her voice again, she asked, "Will his testimony make the difference we need?"

He nodded. "Packard has an entire legal team, but I think Farr's testimony will make the difference."

"This is really good news." Sasha felt immensely relieved. "Thank you."

Silence lingered between them for a moment. When Sasha could bear this new anticipation no longer, she asked, "Did you make your decision?"

He nodded. "I did."

She held her breath. She had no right to expect Branch to alter his life plan for her or for Brianne.

"I'm staying in Winchester."

Relief whooshed through her. "I'm sure your parents and your grandmother are thrilled."

"They are." He grinned. "To be honest, I'm really

happy about the decision. It wasn't an easy one to make but it feels right."

"I'm glad."

He held her gaze for a moment. "Good to know."

They were dancing all around this thing between them, but right now neither of them could emotionally afford to go there. They both needed time.

"I've taken a leave of absence to take care of things around here, so I'm not going anywhere for a while either."

"Sounds like a smart plan."

His tone was guarded. Was he worried about where they went from here? Frankly, she was definitely worried but they had other considerations—like a preteen daughter.

"I think so. I want to stay close—at least for a while. Give you a chance to get to know your daughter."

The anticipation that lit in his eyes made her heart skip a beat.

"I'd like that a lot."

Sasha nodded. "Good, because she can't wait to meet you."

Brianne was giddy with excitement. She couldn't wait to learn all about the other half of her family.

A grin peeked past his guarded facade. "The feeling is definitely mutual."

Branch and Brianne had spoken by phone every day. As soon as the plane landed yesterday she'd wanted to drive straight to his house, but Sasha had insisted on her taking a moment to acclimate herself.

"Would you like to come in and say hello in person?"

He nodded. "I would."

They walked up the front steps together. He reached to open the door and she hesitated. "I wondered if you might like to come to dinner tonight. Brianne and I are cooking."

"Name the place and time."

"Seven, at my grandmother's?"

He gave a nod. "I'll be there."

He opened the door and Sasha walked in ahead of him. Brianne was loping down the stairs.

"Hey, sweetie, this—" she gestured to the man next to her "—is Branch."

Brianne stood on the bottom step for a long moment while she took in the real-life man who was her father.

Branch broke the ice by stepping forward and extending his hand. "It's very nice to meet you in person, Brianne."

She put her hand in his and gave it a shake. "Nice to meet you."

"Brianne and I were about to take a walk. Maybe you'd like to join us."

"Sure."

They walked back outside and wandered across the yard. Sasha hung back to watch the two of them together. It was amazing how much Brianne looked like her father. Sasha had known but it was so much more evident in person. She also understood that this fledgling relationship would not be so easy every day. Right now her daughter was in the honeymoon phase of this new discovery. There would be bumps in the road along the way, but for now they were both committed to building a solid relationship. Sasha was immensely grateful things were progressing so well.

The dark clouds that had hung over her life for so very long were gone.

Moving into the future had never looked brighter.

Even as the thought whispered through her mind, Branch turned back to her and smiled.

If there had been any question in her heart, she now knew with certainty that this really was home.

Whatever the future held, Branch and Winchester would be a part of it.

* * * * *

*Read on for a special excerpt of
the first book in
The Undertaker's Daughter series,*
Secrets the Dead Keep,
*coming in April from
Debra Webb and MIRA Books!*

Chapter One

Winchester, Tennessee
Monday, May 6, 7:15 a.m.

Mothers shouldn't die this close to Mother's Day.

Especially mothers whose daughters, despite being grown and having families of their own, still considered Mom to be their best friend. Rowan Du-Pont had spent the better part of last night consoling the daughters of Geneva Phillips. Geneva had failed to show at church on Sunday morning, and later that same afternoon she wasn't answering her cell, so the younger daughter entered her mother's home and found her deceased in the bathtub.

Now the seventy-two-year-old woman's body waited in refrigeration for Rowan to begin the preparations for her final journey. The viewing wasn't until tomorrow evening, so there was no particular rush. The husband of one of the daughters was on business in London and wouldn't arrive back home until late today. There was time for a short break, which turned into a morning drive that had taken

Rowan across town and to a place she hadn't visited in better than two decades.

Like death, some things were inevitable. Coming back to this place was one of those things. Perhaps it was the hours spent with the sisters last night that had prompted memories of Rowan's own sister. She and her twin had once been inseparable. Wasn't that generally the way with identical twins?

The breeze shifted, lifting a wisp of hair across her face. Rowan swiped it away and stared out over Tims Ford Lake. The dark, murky waters spread like sprawling arms some thirty-odd miles upstream from the nearby dam, enveloping the treacherous Elk River in its embrace. The water was deep and unforgiving. Even standing on the bank, at least ten feet from the edge, a chill crept up Rowan's spine. She hated this place. Hated the water. The ripples that broke the shadowy surface…the smell of fish and rotting plant life. She hated every little thing about it.

This was the spot where her sister's body had been found.

July sixth, twenty-seven years ago. Rowan and her twin sister, Raven, had turned twelve years old that spring. Rowan's gaze lingered on the decaying tree trunk and the cluster of newer branches and overgrowth stretching from the bank into the hungry water where her sister's lifeless body had snagged. The current had dragged her pale, thin body a good distance before depositing her at this spot. It had taken eight hours and twenty-three minutes for the search teams to find her.

Rowan had known her sister was dead before the call had come that Raven had gone missing. Her parents had rushed to help with the search, leaving a neighbor with Rowan. She had stood at her bedroom window watching for their return. The house had felt completely empty and Rowan had understood that her life would never be the same.

No matter that nearly three decades had passed since that sultry summer day, she could still recall the horrifying feel of the final tug, and then the ominous release of her sister's physical presence.

She shifted her gaze from the water to the sky. Last night the temperature had taken an unseasonable plunge. Blackberry winter, the locals called it. Whether it held some glimmer of basis in botany or was merely rooted in folklore, blackberry bushes all over the county were in full bloom. Rowan pulled her sweater tight around her. Though today was the first time she had come to this place since returning home, the dark water was never far from her thoughts. How could it be? The lake swelled and withdrew around Winchester like the rhythmic breath of a sleeping giant, at once harmless and menacing.

Rowan had sneaked away to this spot dozens of times after her sister was buried. Other times she had ridden her bike to the cemetery and visited her there or simply sat in Raven's room and stared at the bed where she had once laid her head. But Rowan felt closest to her sister here, near the water that had snatched her life away like the merciless talons of a hawk descending on a fleeing field mouse.

"You should have stayed home," Rowan murmured to herself. The ache, no matter the many years that had passed, twisted in her chest.

She had begged Raven not to go to the party. Her sister had been convinced that Rowan's behavior was nothing more than jealousy since she hadn't been invited. The suggestion hadn't been entirely unjustified, but mostly Rowan had felt a suffocating dread, a panic that had bordered on hysteria. She had needed her sister to stay home. Every adolescent instinct she possessed had been screaming and restless with that looming sense of trepidation.

But Raven had ignored her sister's pleas and attended the big barbecue and swim party with her best friend, Tessa Cardwell, and the rest was history.

Rowan exhaled a beleaguered breath. At moments like this she felt exactly as if her life was moving backward. She'd enjoyed a fulfilling career with the Metropolitan Nashville Police Department as an adviser for the special crimes unit. As a psychiatrist, she had found her work immensely satisfying and she had helped to solve numerous homicide cases. But then, not quite two months ago, everything had changed. The one case that Rowan didn't recognize had been happening right in front of her, shattering her life…and sending everything spiraling out of control.

The life she had built in Nashville had been comfortable, with enough intellectual challenge in her career to make it uniquely interesting. Though she had not possessed a gold shield, the detectives in the special crimes unit had valued her opinion and treated her as if she was as much a member of the team as any of them. But that was before...*before* the man she admired and trusted proved to be a serial killer—a killer who murdered her father and an MNPD officer as well as more than a hundred other victims over the past several decades.

A mere one month, twenty-two days and about fourteen hours ago esteemed psychiatrist Dr. Julian Addington emerged from his cloak of secrecy and changed the way the world viewed serial killers. He was the first of his kind: incredibly prolific, cognitively brilliant and innately chameleonlike—able to change his MO at will. Far too clever to hunt among his own patients or social set, he had chosen his victims carefully, always ensuring he or she could never be traced back to him or his life.

Julian had fooled Rowan for the past two decades and then he'd taken her father, her only remaining family, from her. He'd devastated and humiliated her both personally and professionally.

Anger and loathing churned inside her. He wanted her to suffer. He wanted her to be defeated...to give up. But she would not. Determination solidified inside her. She would not allow him that victory or that level of control over her.

Her gaze drifted out over the water once more. Since her father's death and moving back to Winchester, people had asked her dozens of times why she'd returned to take over the funeral home after

all these years. She always gave the same answer—
I'm a DuPont. It's what we do.

Her father, of course, had always hoped Rowan
would do so. It was the DuPont way. The funeral
home had been in the family for a hundred and fifty
years; the legacy had been passed from one generation to the next time and time again. When she'd
graduated from college and chosen to go to medical school and become a psychiatrist rather than to
return home and take over the family business, Edward DuPont had been shattered. For more than a
year after that decision she and her father had been
estranged. Now she mourned that lost year with an
ache that was soul deep.

They had reconciled, she reminded herself, and
other than the perpetual guilt she felt over not visit-
ing or calling often enough, things had been good
between her and her father. Like all else in her life
until recently, their relationship had been comfortable. They'd spoken by phone regularly. She missed
those chats. He kept her up to speed on who married or moved or passed and she would tell him as
much as she could about her latest case. He had loved
hearing about her work with Metro. As much as he'd
wanted her to take over the family legacy, he had
wished for her to be happy more than anything else.

"I miss you, Daddy," she murmured.

Looking back, Rowan deeply regretted having
allowed Julian Addington to become a part of her
life all those years ago. She had shared her deepest,
darkest secrets with him, including her previously

strained relationship with her father. She had purged years of pent-up frustrations and anxieties to the bastard first as his patient and then, later, as a colleague and friend.

Though logic told her otherwise, a part of her would always feel the weight of responsibility for her father's murder.

Due to her inability to see what Julian was, she could not possibly return to Metro though they had assured her that there would always be a place for her in the department. How could she dare to pretend some knowledge or insight the detectives themselves did not possess when she had unknowingly been a close friend to one of the most prolific serial killers the world had ever known?

She could not. *This* was her life now.

Would taking over the family business completely assuage the guilt she felt for letting her father down all those years ago? Certainly not. Never. But it was what she had to do. It was her destiny. In truth, she had started to regret her career decision well before her father's murder. Perhaps it was the approaching age milestone of forty or simply a midlife crisis. She had found herself pondering what might have been different if she'd made that choice and regretting, frankly, that she hadn't.

Since she and Raven were old enough to follow the simplest directions, they had been trained to prepare a body for its final journey. By the time they were twelve, they could carry out the necessary steps nearly as well as their father with little or no direction.

Growing up surrounded by death had, of course, left its mark. Her hyperawareness of death and all its ripples and aftershocks made putting so much stock into a relationship with another human being a less than attractive proposal. Why go out of her way to risk that level of pain in the event that person was lost? And with life came loss. To that end, she would likely never marry or have children. But she had her work and, like her father, she intended to do her very best. Both of them had always been workaholics. Taking care of the dead was a somber, albeit important, task, particularly for those left behind. The families of the loved ones who passed through the DuPont doors looked to her for support and guidance during their time of sorrow and emotional turmoil.

Speaking of which, she pulled her cell from her pocket and checked the time. She should get back to the funeral home. Mrs. Phillips was waiting. Rowan turned away from the part of her past that still felt fresh despite the passage of time.

Along this part of the shore the landscape was thickly wooded and dense with undergrowth, which was the reason she'd worn her yard-mucking boots and was slowly picking her way back to the road. As she attempted to slide her phone back into her hip pocket a limb snagged her hair. Instinctively she reached up to pull it loose, dropping her cell phone in the process.

"Damn it." Rowan reached down and felt through the thatch beneath the underbrush. More long blond strands caught in the brush. She should have taken the time to put her hair in a ponytail as she usually did. She tugged it loose, bundled the thick mass into her left hand and then crouched down to dig around with her right in search of her phone. Like most people, she felt utterly lost without the damn thing.

Where the hell had it fallen?

She would have left it in the car except that she never wanted a family member to call the funeral home and reach a machine. With that in mind, she forwarded calls to her cell when she was away. Eventually she hoped to trust her father's new assistant director enough to allow him to handle all incoming calls. Wouldn't have helped this morning since he was on vacation.

New assistant director? She almost laughed at the idea. Woody Holder had been with her father for two years, but Herman Carter had been with him a lifetime before that. She supposed in comparison *new* was a reasonable way of looking at Woody's tenure thus far. Her father had still referred to him as the new guy. Maybe it was his lackadaisical attitude. At forty-five Woody appeared to possess absolutely no ambition and very little motivation. She really should consider finding a new, more dependable assistant director and letting Woody go.

Her fingers raked through the leaves and decaying ground cover until she encountered something cool and hard but not metal or plastic. Definitely not her phone. She stilled, frowned in concentration as her sense of touch attempted to identify the object she couldn't see without sticking her head into the bushes. Not happening. She might have chalked the object up to being a limb or a rock if not for the familiar, tingling sensation rushing along every single nerve ending in her body. Her instincts were humming fiercely.

Assuredly not a rock.

Holding her breath, she reached back to the same spot and touched the object again. Her fingers dug into the soft earth around the object and curled instinctively.

Long. Narrow. Cylindrical.

She pulled it from the rich, soft dirt, the thriving moss and the tangle of rotting leaves.

Bone.

She frowned, studied it closely. *Human* bone.

Her pulse tripped into a faster rhythm. She placed the bone aside and reached back in with both hands and carefully scratched away more of the leaves.

Another bone…and then another. Bones that, judging by their condition, had been here for a very long time.

Meticulously sifting through the layers of leaves and plant life, she discovered that her cell phone had fallen into the rib cage. The *human* rib cage. Her mind racing with questions and conclusions, she cautiously fished out the phone. She took a breath, hit her contacts list and tapped the name of Winchester's chief of police.

When he picked up, rather than *hello*, she said, "I'm at the lake. There's something here you need to see and it can't wait. Better call Burt and send him in this direction, as well." Burt Johnston was a local veterinarian who had served as the county coroner for as long as Rowan could remember.

Chief of Police William "Billy" Brannigan's first response was "Are *you* okay?"

Rowan had been wrong when she'd considered that without her father she was alone. There was Billy—the two of them had been friends since grade school. And there was Herman. He was more like an uncle than a mere friend. Eventually she hoped the two of them would stop worrying so about her. She wasn't that fragile young girl who had left Winchester twenty-odd years ago. Recent events had rocked her, that was true, but she was completely capable of taking care of herself. She had made sure she would never again be vulnerable to anyone.

"I'm fine but someone's not. You should stop worrying about me and get over here, Billy."

"I'm on my way."

She ended the call. There had been no need for her to tell him precisely where she was at the lake. He would know. Rowan DuPont didn't swim and she never came near the lake unless it was to visit her sister.

Strange, all those times Rowan had come to visit Raven she'd never realized there was someone else here, too.

Pick up Secrets the Dead Keep, *the first title in*
The Undertaker's Daughter series
by Debra Webb.

Available April 2019!

Get 4 FREE REWARDS!

We'll send you 2 FREE Books plus 2 FREE Mystery Gifts.

Harlequin Intrigue® books feature heroes and heroines that confront and survive danger while finding themselves irresistibly drawn to one another.

FREE
Value Over
$20

Declan O'Neill hiked his rucksack higher on his shoulders
and trudged down the sidewalk in downtown Washington,
DC. The last time he'd seen so many people in one place,
he'd been a fresh recruit at US Marine Corps basic training
in San Diego, California, standing among a bunch of
teenagers, just like him, being processed into the military.

He shouldered his way through the throngs of
sightseers, businessmen and career women hurrying to the
next building along the road. The sun shone on a bright
spring day. Cherry blossoms exploded in fluffy pinkish-
white, dripping petals onto the lawns and sidewalks in an
optimistic display of hope.

Hope.

Declan snorted. Here he was, eleven years after joining
the US Marine Corps…eleven years of knowing what was
expected of him, of not having to decide what to wear each
day. Eleven years of a steady paycheck, no matter how

small, in an honorable profession, making a difference in the world.

Now he was faced with the daunting task of job hunting with a huge strike on his record.

But not today.

Why he'd decided to take the train from Bethesda, Maryland, to the political hub of the entire country was beyond his own comprehension. But with nowhere else to go and nothing holding him back—no job, no family, no home—he'd thought, "Why not?"

He'd never been to the White House, never stopped to admire the Declaration of Independence, drafted by the forefathers of his country and he'd never stood at the foot of the Lincoln Memorial, in the shadow of the likeness of Abraham Lincoln, a leader who'd set the United States on a revolutionary course. He'd never been to the Vietnam War Memorial or any other memorial in DC.

Yeah. And so what?

Sightseeing wouldn't pay the bills. Out of the military, out of money and sporting a dishonorable discharge, Declan would be hard-pressed to find a decent job. Who would hire a man whose only skills were superb marksmanship that allowed him to kill a man from four hundred yards away, expertise in hand-to-hand combat and the ability to navigate himself out of a paper bag with nothing more than the stars and his wits?

Need an adrenaline rush from nail-biting tales
(and irresistible males)?

Check out **Harlequin Intrigue**®,
Harlequin® **Romantic Suspense** and
Love Inspired® **Suspense** books!

New books available every month!

CONNECT WITH US AT:

Facebook.com/groups/HarlequinConnection

Facebook.com/HarlequinBooks

Twitter.com/HarlequinBooks

Instagram.com/HarlequinBooks

Pinterest.com/HarlequinBooks

ReaderService.com

**ROMANCE WHEN
YOU NEED IT**

A blizzard is keeping guests at Sterling Montana Guest Ranch, where a killer is lurking in the shadows.

Read on for a sneak preview of
Stroke of Luck *by* New York Times *and* USA TODAY
bestselling author B.J. Daniels.

"Bad luck always comes in threes."

Standing in the large kitchen of the Sterling Montana Guest Ranch, Will Sterling shot the woman an impatient look. "I don't have time for this right now, Dorothea."

"Just sayin'," Dorothea Brand muttered under her breath. The fifty-year-old housekeeper was short and stout with a helmet of dark hair and piercing dark eyes. She'd been a fixture on the ranch since Will and his brothers were kids, which made her invaluable, but also as bossy as an old mother hen.

After the Sterling boys had lost their mother, Dorothea had stepped in. Their father, Wyatt, had continued to run the guest ranch alone and then with the help of his sons until his death last year. For the first time, Will would finally be running the guest ranch without his father calling all the shots. He'd been looking forward to the challenge and to carrying on the family business.

But now his cook was laid up with a broken leg? He definitely didn't like the way the season was starting, Will thought as the housekeeper leaned against the counter, giving him one of her you're-going-to-regret-this looks as he considered who he could call.

As his brother Garrett brought in a box of supplies from town, Will asked, "Do you know anyone who can cook?"

"What about Poppy Carmichael?" Garrett suggested as he pulled a bottle of water from the refrigerator, opened it and took a long drink. "She's a caterer now."

Will frowned. "Poppy?" An image appeared of a girl with freckles, braces, skinned knees and reddish-brown hair in pigtails. "I haven't thought of Poppy in years. I thought she moved away."

"She did, but she came back about six months ago and started a catering business in Whitefish," Garrett said. "I only know because I ran into her at a party recently. The food was really good, if that helps."

"Wait, I remember her. Cute kid. Didn't her father work for the forest service?" their younger brother Shade asked as he also came into the kitchen with a box of supplies. He deposited the box inside the large pantry just off the kitchen. "Last box," he announced, dusting off his hands.

"You remember, Will. Poppy and her dad lived in the old forest service cabin a mile or so from here," Garrett said, grinning at him. "She used to ride her bike over here and help us with our chores. At least, that was her excuse."

Will avoided his brother's gaze. It wasn't like he'd ever forgotten.

"I just remember the day she decided to ride Lightning," Shade said. "She climbed up on the corral, and as the horse ran by, she jumped on it!" He shook his head, clearly filled with admiration. "I can't imagine what she thought she was going to do, riding him bareback." He laughed. "She stayed on a lot longer than I thought she would. But it's a wonder she didn't kill herself. The girl had grit. But I always wondered what possessed her to do that."

Garrett laughed and shot another look at Will. "She was trying to impress our brother."

"That poor little girl was smitten," Dorothea agreed as she narrowed her dark gaze at Will. "And you, being fifteen and full of yourself, often didn't give her the time of day. So what could possibly go wrong hiring her to cook for you?"

Don't miss
Stroke of Luck *by B.J. Daniels, available March 2019*
wherever HQN Books and ebooks are sold.

www.Harlequin.com

PHBJDEXP0319

Love Harlequin romance?

DISCOVER.

Be the first to find out about promotions, news and exclusive content!

 Facebook.com/HarlequinBooks

 Twitter.com/HarlequinBooks

 Instagram.com/HarlequinBooks

 Pinterest.com/HarlequinBooks

ReaderService.com

EXPLORE.

Sign up for the Harlequin e-newsletter and download a free book from any series at **TryHarlequin.com.**

CONNECT.

Join our Harlequin community to share your thoughts and connect with other romance readers!
Facebook.com/groups/HarlequinConnection

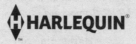

HARLEQUIN®

ROMANCE WHEN
YOU NEED IT

HSOCIAL2018